YEARS
of pure reading pleasure

GW00342037

100 Reasons to Celebrate

We invite you to join us in celebrating
Mills & Boon's centenary. Gerald Mills and
Charles Boon founded Mills & Boon Limited
in 1908 and opened offices in London's Covent
Garden. Since then, Mills & Boon has become
a hallmark for romantic fiction, recognised
around the world.

We're proud of our 100 years of publishing
excellence, which wouldn't have been achieved
without the loyalty and enthusiasm of our
authors and readers.

Thank you!

Each month throughout the year there will
be something new and exciting to mark the
centenary, so watch for your favourite authors,
captivating new stories, special limited
edition collections...and more!

Dear Reader

One of my fondest memories is slithering under the spare bed at my grandmother's house and finding an ever evolving treasure trove of Mills & Boon books. Hundreds of them. Dog-eared, much-loved, and waiting for me, the next generation of romance reader, to discover them.

I have kept a handful of those books, some of which must be well over twenty years old by now, in a treasure chest in my childhood bedroom alongside my high-school flute, old dancing costumes, and my first teddy bear, because they are all markers of moments in time in my life.

Mills & Boon have been a part of my reading life for as long as I can remember, and when I first set out to write a book there was no doubt as to where I hoped that book's home would be. So, a great big thanks to Mills & Boon for allowing me to become part of the family, and congratulations on your first one hundred years!

Ally
www.allyblake.com

FALLING FOR
THE REBEL HEIR

BY
ALLY BLAKE

⊚™ MILLS & BOON®
Pure reading pleasure

First published in Great Britain 2008
Harlequin Mills & Boon Limited,
Eton House, 18-24 Paradise Road, Richmond, Surrey TW9 1SR

© Ally Blake 2008

ISBN: 978 0 263 86503 5

Set in Times Roman 13 on 14½ pt
02-0308-53232

Printed and bound in Spain
by Litografia Rosés, S.A., Barcelona

Having once been a professional cheerleader, **Ally Blake's** motto is 'Smile and the world smiles with you.' One way to make Ally smile is by sending her on holidays, especially to locations which inspire her writing. New York and Italy are by far her favourite destinations. Other things that make her smile are the gracious city of Melbourne, the gritty Collingwood football team, and her gorgeous husband Mark.

Reading romance novels was a smile-worthy pursuit from long back. So, with such valuable preparation already behind her, she wrote and sold her first book. Her career as a writer also gives her a perfectly reasonable excuse to indulge in her stationery addiction. That alone is enough to keep her grinning every day! Ally would love you to visit her at her website www.allyblake.com

For two of the loveliest women I've ever known.

Dell and Barbara: godmothers and friends.

CHAPTER ONE

HUD hitched his dilapidated rucksack higher on to his shoulder as he stood staring at the façade of Claudel, the grand old house before him.

Ivy trailed over masonry outer walls, the front marble steps were steeped in mould, the delicately framed picture windows were layered in many years' worth of storm-splattered mud, the multi-gabled grey roof was now missing tiles and the gutters were filled with rotting leaves.

But even a decade's worth of invading shabbiness couldn't stop the memories of sunny days spent with his aunt in the big house from melting into one another—a dozen summers during which his parents had taken off on adventures to far-flung lands to authenticate new discoveries about old civilisations, leaving him behind. He pictured himself lying in the cool grass at the side of the house reading Aunt Fay's original editions of *The Chronicles of Narnia*, wishing himself a faun or a lion or, even better, one of the four Pevensie brothers and sisters taking part in adventures. Together.

He sniffed in deep through his nose, then, leaving the house and its deluge of memories for later, he hooked a sharp left to head into Claudel's colossal garden, only to discover far sorrier disarray.

What had once been a perfect green lawn, littered with croquet arches and bordered by a dramatic garden boasting random marble sculptures worthy of any gallery, was now overgrown weed-infested chaos. Once immaculately clipped conifers were now untamed, with patches torn apart by storms leaving raw-looking wounds. Chickweed, blackberries and roses ran wild. Any patch of grass still visible through the shrubs was littered with wild daisies. Had Aunt Fay been alive to see how much he'd let the place go, she would have screamed bloody murder.

But, after the initial shock wore off, Hud began to notice that the air had been made pungent with a rich floral scent, and through the gaps in the undergrowth bees and wattle dust floated on the hazy summer air. As a photographer for Voyager Enterprises, for both their documentary TV channel and magazine, he'd shot the gardens of queens, rainforests which by now had been demolished and thick, viny, mystical swamps protected by rednecks with guns. But this place was so out of control, so uncontaminated and crazy beautiful, Hud's throat clogged with unexpected emotion.

He cleared his throat, shoved the feelings down deep inside him where he'd kept every other come-from-out-of-nowhere and too-hard-to-deal-with-right-now feeling that had threatened to expose him over the past couple of months and moved on, forward through the undergrowth, not much caring that branches scratched at his hands or that his jeans collected spiky thorns. It only brought back more memories of trailing Aunt Fay's crazy Irish wolfhound through the same gardens as the dog in turn had chased invisible air sprites.

Through a gap in the seemingly never-ending wilderness, Hud was blinded by a pinpoint of light. He held up a hand to shield his eyes and tugged his rucksack through the heavy undergrowth until he found himself face to face with the old pool house.

A half smile tugged at the corners of his mouth and pressed against the backs of his tired eyes as echoes of more long forgotten recollections tickled at the corner of his mind. Dive bombing. Performing pretty darned legendary back flips off the diving board. Lying on his back in the water for hours simply watching clouds shift past the pitched glass roof, wondering if his mum and dad looked up they would see the same clouds while trekking some thrilling spot on the other side of the world.

Back then he'd been full of hope and plans that when he grew up, when he was old enough to set out on his own life adventure, then he'd finally understand what the fuss was all about. Why it had been so easy for his parents to leave him behind. He wondered when all that impenetrable hope had become frustration. When anticipation had become cold knowledge. When he had grown up after all.

Had it been hiding with only his camera for company beneath a bush for eighteen hours in the middle of a shoot-out in Bosnia when he had barely been twenty-one? Waking to find that his team had been abandoned by their guide at Base Camp on K2 on his twenty-sixth birthday? Or when he'd woken in a London hospital less than two months earlier, barely strong enough to ask for a glass of water?

He levered his heavy rucksack to the ground and left it where it lay. Claudel was fifty metres off the road, behind a ten foot brick wall and a ten minute walk through a pine forest to the nearby township of Saffron. If anybody was lucky enough to find his shabby old khaki bag they were welcome to the raggedy clothes and just as threadbare passport within. It wasn't as though he'd be needing them to head through a different kind of wilderness with his trusty Nikon camera slung over one shoulder and a hunting knife slung over the other with his team of documentary film-makers at his back any time soon.

He cricked his neck, pressed his hands into the tight small of his back and glanced upwards to find brilliant red bougainvillea creepers seemed to have swallowed half the long building, leaving the hundred odd remaining white-framed glass panels that had survived the test of time thick with dust and mould. He could only hazard a guess how foul the inside might be after not having been blessed by a human touch for a good ten years.

'If memory serves correctly…' he said out loud, the sound of his voice raspy and deep in his ears after hours of non-use. Then he made his way around the back of the building to find the door was ajar, at an odd angle, askew on rusted hinges, as though it had been yanked open.

With instinct born of years spent stepping un-announced into dark, secret places, he stepped quietly—toe to heel—over a small pile of worn broken glass and inside the pool house where his feet came to a giveaway scraping halt of boot soles on tessellated French tiles.

The pool house was clean. The mottled green tiles around the margins sparkled and the dozen white marble benches were spotless. Miniature palm trees in plant boxes edging the length of the room were luscious with good health. And the water in the pool shimmered dark and inviting against the black-painted concrete bottom.

A sound broke through Hud's reverie. A soft ripple as water lapped gently against the edge of the pool. And he was hit with the sense that something was about to break the dark surface. He held his breath, squared his stance, squinted into the shadows and watched in practised silence as…

A mermaid rose from the depths.

From there everything seemed to slow—his breathing, his heartbeat, the dust floating through shards of sunlight, as the nymph sliced through the water, away from him, leaving a trail of leisurely wavelets in her wake.

Water streamed over hair the colour of brandy. It ran adoringly over pale, lean, youthful arms. And, as she swayed up the steps, water gripped her willowy form as long as it could before cruel gravity claimed it back to the dark depths.

Hud felt as if he ought to avert his gaze. As if he was too old, too cynical, too jaded to be allowed such a vision. But those same qualities only meant that his curiosity far outweighed his humility, and his eyes remained riveted to the back of the exquisite stranger.

Once she was land bound her hair sprang into heavy waves that reached all the way to the small of her back, covering the expanse of skin left visible by her simple swimsuit. It was functional. Black. One piece. But, with its low-cut back and high-cut leg, the whole thing was just sexy enough that Hud's pulse beat so loudly in his ears he feared she might hear it too.

Her feet made soft slapping sounds as she padded over to grab a soft peach-coloured Paisley-patterned towel draped over the far marble bench, revealing a bundle of clothes beneath.

She then lifted a foot and bent over to run the soft towel down one leg. One long lean leg. A drip of sweat slithered slowly down Hud's cheek.

When she repeated the action with the other leg, her movements relaxed and unhurried, he closed his eyes and swallowed to ease his suddenly dry throat.

She lifted the towel and ran it slowly over her hair, wringing out the bulk of the moisture, kicking out her right hip as she did so. Several golden beams of light slicing through the windows above picked up the rich colour of her dark red hair. Dappled sunshine played across her milky skin like a caress. And all Hud could think was that if this wasn't a moment that needed to be captured on film for all eternity, then he didn't know what was.

He was so taken by the aesthetics, mentally calculating focal length and film speed, that he didn't actually notice her begin to spin to face him until it was too late.

She turned. She saw him. And she screamed.

And he didn't half blame her. He hadn't shaved in a fortnight. He was wearing clothes better suited to a London winter than to the thirty degree Melbourne heat.

And she was trespassing on his land and, by the looks of the place, had been for some time.

Kendall yanked her towel to cover her bare legs in a movement that was pure instinct as her scream echoed around the lofty room, bouncing off the glass and back again before sighing to an embarrassing memory.

Unfortunately it hadn't sent the intruder running for his life. He simply continued staring back at her. Tall, swarthy, fully dressed and all male.

As his eyes glanced from one end of her body to the other, she realised that clutching her towel like some maiden wasn't going to help at all. She turned her left side away from him and swirled the towel around her body. Naturally it fought against her, wanting to ebb when she wanted it to flow, but eventually she managed to cover the bits that needed covering.

She then took a deep shaky breath before calmly informing the man to, 'Get the hell out of here and right now, or I'll scream again, this time so loud the whole town will come running.'

His dark eyes lifted to hers. Connected across fifteen metres of cool dark water. Every inch of skin his gaze touched vibrated as though he'd made actual physical contact. She decided it was a side effect of the shock of being half naked before a complete stranger. Nothing more.

'Don't scream again, please,' he said, his mouth kicking into a pleasant kind of smile. He didn't raise his voice, but he didn't need to. The deep rumble carried easily across the wide space. 'One perforated eardrum is quite enough excitement for one day.'

'So leave, now, and you can save the other one.' She spat a clump of wet hair from her mouth. 'If you're lost I can point you the way back to the main road or through the pine forest back into town.' She glanced over her shoulder in that direction and when she looked back she could have sworn he'd moved closer.

'I'm not lost,' he said.

'Well, you're sure not where you're meant to be. Everything within one hundred metres in each direction of this place is part of a private estate.'

He simply smiled some more, making her wonder if he knew that already. Everybody in Saffron knew. Claudel was owned by the descendants of Lady Fay Bennington, who hadn't bothered with upkeep on the beautiful place since Fay had died a decade earlier. But everybody in Saffron *also* knew everybody else from Saffron, and she'd never seen this guy before. He was the kind of man one wouldn't easily forget.

Tall and broad, with the kind of physique that could block out the sun. And dark. Dark clothes. Dark eyes. Dark curling hair in need of a cut. Dark stubble on his face that had gone past a shadow but had not quite been tamed into anything resembling a civilised beard. She would have thought him homeless in his battered coat, tattered jeans and scuffed boots but there was something in his bearing that made that seem a non sequitur. A kind of shoulders back, elegant stance, glint in the eye thing he had going on that negated every other potent signal bombarding her senses.

She tugged her towel tighter.

He sunk his hands into the pockets of an unseasonably heavy brown coat and definitely moved closer. 'I'm thinking you're the one who ought not to be in here, Miss…'

'My name is none of your damn business, buddy.'

She'd taken self-defence classes since she'd come to town and moved in with Taffy. Two single girls living together, she'd figured better safe than sorry. So she knew it was better to run than to try to make an assailant see reason.

She dropped the towel in order to grab her clothes and then realised she was naked bar a sliver of Lycra covering not all that much skin. So she grabbed the towel again, then used it as a makeshift screen as she hurriedly pulled her long red sundress on over her swimsuit.

It wasn't until her head popped through the neck hole and the dress dragged and twisted uncomfortably against her wet bathing suit that she realised it was inside out and back to front. Too bad. Too late. He was getting nearer.

She grabbed her wet hair and tossed it over her back and it instantly soaked right through to her skin, making her feel clammy as well as anxious and embarrassed and just a little bit intimidated.

'Now, don't come any closer,' she insisted, grabbing her Doc Marten boots and holding them in front of her as if they were some kind of lethal weapon.

For whatever reason that seemed to work. The guy stopped. He held out his hands in front of him. Long-fingered hands. Clean hands. The hands of a gentleman, not a drifter.

'There's no need for any of that,' he said. 'Before you do anything foolish like knock me out with a flying shoe, you should know something.'

She wondered if perhaps he couldn't swim and was worried about falling unconscious into the pool.

She didn't want him to come any closer, she didn't want him to tell on her, but she also didn't want to kill the guy. He was far too good-looking to die.

Feeling ridiculous for even thinking such a thing, she lifted her boots an inch higher. 'And what's that?'

'This,' he said, waving his arm to his left and taking another couple of slow steps her way, 'is all mine.'

Her shoes dropped an inch. 'Yours?'

He nodded. And came nearer. He was close enough now for her to notice a thin scar slicing through his stubble from the edge of his nose to his top lip. She knew about scars and the fact that it was still pink meant it was fairly recent.

Apart from that one flaw, it turned out he had a lovely straight nose and a strong jaw, like one of the statues to be found hidden beneath the dense foliage in Claudel's grounds. Up close his dark hair curled with a delectable just-out-of-bed look. Like some sort of modern day Lord Byron.

But all that was swept aside when she glanced back into his eyes. They were hazel. Deep, dark, enigmatic hazel clashing against the whitest of whites she'd ever seen, framed by long dark lashes. *And all that's best of dark and bright meet in his aspect and his eyes,* she thought.

The guy was in need of a shave and haircut and

a shopping expedition, but he was utterly
gorgeous. So gorgeous she realised she had spent
the past twenty seconds staring, and paraphrasing
Byron, as if she hadn't seen a man this beautiful
before. Up close. In the flesh.

A low, lazy hum of awareness settled in her belly.
No, she thought, feeling more panicky at that
thought than any other so far, *not now. Not like this.
I'm not ready.* Her mind shook back and forth vehe-
mently, which her head would have done if she
hadn't wanted to keep both eyes on every move of
Mr Tall, Dark and Dangerous-To-Her-Equilibrium.

She blinked and thought back to what they had
been arguing about. Had he really just suggested…? She raised her shoes to a battle ready
position again. 'What do you mean it's all yours?'

His enigmatic eyes narrowed slightly and she
bit her lip, hoping he had no clue of the thoughts
streaming unchecked through her obviously
chlorine-addled head.

'My name is Hudson Bennington III. Everyone
just calls me Hud,' he said, holding out his right
hand and continuing to close in on her. 'My Aunt
Fay once lived here. I summered here as a child.
And she left it all to me when she died. Ask in
town if you don't believe me. I'm certain there
will be those who remember.'

She stared at his outstretched hand, then into his

eyes, but she found them far too unsettling so she ignored both and bent to quickly pull her heavy boots on instead, the sudden movement jarring at the rigid muscles in her bad leg. She winced and straightened. She didn't dare waste further time lacing them up.

'Well then, I'd better head back to town right now and double-check,' she said. 'A girl can't be too careful.'

She grabbed her towel and moved around the other side of the pool, away from Hudson Bennington III and his dark eyes, and bedroom hair, and rugged elegance, and gentleman's hands, and disturbing Byronesque handsomeness, towards the exit.

If this guy was who he said he was, if he was back to claim the land as his own, her daily swims would be no more. No more revelling in the bliss of floating, of feeling unencumbered, light and vigorous. And if she'd felt panic earlier, it was nothing compared with the all-encompassing dread that filled her at that thought.

'You don't have to run off just yet,' he said, his deep voice calling after her.

But Kendall spilled out into the bright light and walked as fast as her shaking legs would carry her.

She ducked into the pine forest and looked over her shoulder just the once to find Hud standing outside the pool house looking for her, hands on hips, eyes straining. But she knew this part of the world too well and by now she would be no more than one of a thousand shadows between the trunks.

As she picked up her pace, her persistent limp became more pronounced with each step back to town.

Hud ran a hand over his face and stared into the tree line. He had been hot on her heels as she'd left the pool house and then suddenly…she was gone.

A woman who lived locally. A woman with a mouth and an attitude pluckier than he would have expected in a mermaid if he'd ever given it any thought. A woman who up close had skin like porcelain, eyes the colour of the sky before a storm and hair the colour of red wine.

And a woman who, for the too few minutes she'd been near him, had put out of his mind every single thing he'd come back to Claudel in order to forget.

Kendall hit the edge of the pine forest and stopped to check if anybody was out in the main street of Saffron. She didn't want anyone to see her in an inside out, back to front dress, unlaced shoes and sopping wet hair.

It had taken almost all of the three years she'd lived in Saffron for the locals to look past the limp and get over whispering behind their hands about how it had happened. The car accident. A young man's death. Her missing months afterwards. Now she had become the steady, dependable, sensible fact checker for the local newspaper. And she was determined to keep it that way.

When she spotted a break in the dawdling morning traffic she looked right, then left, then right again, before darting across Peach Street, through the garden gate and into the two-storey cottage she shared with Taffy.

The noise she made kicking off her shoes and throwing her wet towel over the back of a chair in the hall was enough for Taffy to look up from her spot at the kitchen table. Her Sunday newspaper dropped in a show of slow motion dawning, her eyes grew wide as saucers and she coughed on her honey-covered English muffin. 'What on earth happened to you?'

'I don't want to talk about it.' Kendall continued up the stairs. She wished she could take them two at a time, but she'd walked so fast into town her damn leg now thrummed.

'Oh, no, you don't.' Taffy's voice slunk up the stairs behind her, followed by thunderously healthy footsteps.

Kendall burst into her room. Her deaf schnauzer, Orlando, looked up at the flurry of movement and then dropped his sweet snout back on to his paws.

Taffy came into Kendall's bedroom and leant against the door-jamb, hooking one bare foot along the other calf. 'So,' she said, 'was there a sudden rainstorm? At the market? Because that's where you told me you were going, remember. To the market to look for fresh meat for tonight's dinner.'

'And…' Kendall said, twisting her damp hair into a low bun and searching madly through the pile of washing on the tub chair in the corner of her room for a fresh towel.

'And… I see no evidence of meat. Only wet hair and a dress that seems to be inside out.' Taffy spilled into the room, her hand to her heart. 'Oh, Kendall! Please tell me fresh meat was code for—'

Kendall threw up her hands and screwed up her eyes to cut out the disturbing images in her head—images of a tanned forearm, a sinewy wrist with a smattering of dark hair and a watch that looked as if it had lived through three world wars. 'Taffy! Stop!'

Taffy sat on the corner of Kendall's bed and licked honey off her fingers. She then buttoned her lip and waited for Kendall to simply talk.

Sick of feeling like a bedraggled cat, Kendall

tore her dress over her head and wrapped herself in the towel, feeling strangely as if she were back in the pool house again. On show. She didn't like it. Once upon a time she'd revelled in it. Being the centre of attention. The class clown. Not any more. 'Do you want to go out while I get changed?'

Taffy shook her head. 'Tell me about the meat.'

Kendall's instinct was for self-protection. But this was Taffy. Taffy who'd taken her in at the time in her life when she'd most needed a friend, when the family she'd come to love as her own had left her out in the cold. Besides, she'd already been sprung by the one person who meant her secret getaway couldn't be a secret any more.

She slumped down on to the bed next to her friend. 'I was swimming.'

'At the falls?'

'No. At Claudel.'

'The old house? But how? The place is decrepit.'

Kendall shrugged. 'Not so much. Not the pool house at least. Not any more.'

Taffy shook her head and half laughed at the same time. 'What have you done now?'

Kendall leant over and buried her face in her palms. 'I found it on one of my forest walks. It's the most beautiful building, Taff. And it was just so sad seeing it falling apart like it was. I got this crazy compulsion to make it like new again. Now

I've cleaned the place up, the floor tiles look like bottled glass. And the marble benches are like something out of a Grace Kelly movie.'

'Whoa, back up a sec. You cleaned?'

Kendall laughed into her hands, then sat up straight, unpeeling her hands from her face. 'I more than cleaned, Taff. I filled it. Chlorinated it. Kept it pristine. Perfect. And visited every day for the past two years. The moment I saw it, I kind of just…had no choice.'

'But that still doesn't quite explain this.' Taffy grabbed a hunk of Kendall's hair and let it slap against her back.

'Today…' Kendall said, then took a deep breath as she tried to find the words to explain the unexpected effect of tall, dark ruggedness without making an idiot of herself. 'Today I was sprung. By Claudel's owner.'

After a long silence, Taffy said, 'Don't tell me you mean Hud?'

Kendall looked her friend in the eye for the first time since she'd got home. 'Hudson Bennington. The third, no less.'

Taffy slapped her on the arm. Then once more for good measure. 'Get out of here.'

'I would love to, but you won't let me. You know him?'

'God, yeah. I had the hugest crush on Hud Bennington when he was eighteen and I was thirteen. It was his last year of boarding school and he was here for the summer, staying with Fay while his folks scooted off to Latvia in search of leprechaun remains or something. He was my teen idol if it's possible for a real life human to be such a thing. So what was he like? All feisty and charming? Cheeky? Pathologically flirtatious? Dry wit? Still as big and gorgeous as ever?'

'He…he looked like he needed a shave.' *And more*, Kendall thought. *He looked like he needed a hug*.

'Ooh,' Taffy said. 'Stubble on Hud Bennington. That I just have to see. Now hurry up and get dressed and you can go right back over there and reintroduce me.'

The thought of coming face to face with all that undomesticated manhood sent a warning note through Kendall. 'Did you not hear me?' she said. 'He caught me. In his pool. Without his permission. Or prior knowledge. While I was naked *bar…my…swimmers*.'

Which for another woman would have been a tad awkward, or for Taffy would have amounted to as good an introduction to a cute guy as she could hope for, but for Kendall that meant something wholly different.

Taffy smiled and nodded like a simpleton. But

Kendall knew she was anything but simple. Tenacious, clever and stubborn was her Taffy.

'Go over there yourself if you like,' Kendall said. 'I'm not going to stop you. Just don't tell the guy you know me and you'll be peachy.'

'Nah,' Taffy said, 'that would seem too eager. Much better to casually bump into him in town. Offer him a coffee so that we can reminisce. And he can remember how I followed him around like a puppy that summer.' Taffy dragged herself off the bed with a groan. 'Or maybe I'll never leave the house again and the men the world over can breathe a sigh of relief that I'm still on the market. Now, get out of here, you're leaving a wet patch on your bed.'

Taffy left. And Kendall took herself, her bedraggled hair and her damp swimsuit out of the door and into the bathroom, where she spent the next half an hour sitting on the bottom of the shower, letting the warm water run over her clammy skin as the shakes that had threatened the moment she had been discovered finally took her over.

She ran a hand down her damaged left thigh, kneading, hoping it might ease slightly. But it worked as well as putting a Band-Aid on a broken heart.

For the regular aches and pains she felt on a daily basis seemed to have spread. Into her chest.

Deep, throbbing, like a forgotten memory trying to burst through to the surface. She knew what those aches were. It was the bitter-sweet sting of unwelcome attraction. And it terrified her to the tips of her black-painted toenails.

She closed her eyes, revelled in the soothing water and tried desperately not to think too hard about how Hud Bennington's arrival had thrown a spanner into the workings of her neat and tidy life.

An hour later, after reintroducing himself to his old bedroom—still just as he'd left it a dozen years before, with its king-sized bed, boxy teak furniture and small aeroplanes on the wallpaper—Hud stood under the wide brass showerhead in his old bathroom, amazed that the pipes still worked. Amazed and thankful. The purposely cool water sloughed away the remnant heat he'd carried with him since leaving the airport.

He closed his eyes and opened his mouth and savoured the taste of Melbourne water streaming over his face, bringing with it more memories he'd long forgotten.

Six years old and running away the first night his parents had left him here and getting lost in the pine forest before Aunt Fay found him—she and her neck-to-ankle layers of lace, lolloping dog and hurricane lamp. The hundred-year-old oak tree in the centre of town that he knew had changed every summer he visited though he couldn't see how. The piano in the downstairs parlour with its broken e-flat.

And then suddenly, before he even felt them coming, memories of another kind swarmed over him, making the water in his mouth taste like dust. Memories of *no* water. For days. So thirsty he couldn't stop shaking. And the sound of a dripping tap in a room nearby. So close. Yet achingly out of reach.

His eyes flew open. He switched off the tap, his breath loud in the huge marble shower. He leant his hand against the wall, watching the droplets slide from his skin and drip to the floor. Just as they had when his high-spirited mermaid had sprung forth from the depths of the glimmering pool.

He concentrated on brandy-coloured hair. Long pale limbs. Stormy blue-grey eyes. His breathing settled. His memories calmed. And he only had her to thank for it.

Whoever she was.

CHAPTER TWO

HUD woke early the next morning. While still fuzzy with sleep, he tugged on a pair of old jeans and a T-shirt from the minimal choices still stuffed into his rucksack and headed downstairs, through Claudel's cold, silent rooms and outside into the post-dawn mist.

It wasn't all that long before he found himself swinging by the pool house. He thought about poking his head inside, even though he knew that he'd find nothing there bar still water and lingering shadows. He hadn't led a charitable enough life to deserve stumbling upon such an apparition two days running.

Instead he kept walking until he was swallowed up by the cool dauntingly tall moss-covered trees, flat beige ground covered in a layer of pine needles and shadows of the mighty forest separating Claudel's grounds from the nearby town.

He let his fingers trail over the rough bark, the

tactile discomfort grounding him while he headed he knew not where. Into blissful nothingness? Or with all too specific purpose—the knowledge that this was the last place he had seen *her*?

The sound of a cracking branch stilled his steps. He looked out into the tightly packed trunks and saw something shimmer and shift. Lucky for him this wasn't bear country. Though he'd come to realise that humans could be far worse creatures to stumble upon down a dark alley.

The form stirred. Took shape. Human shape. Female shape. And there she was. As if he had conjured her out of the mist. His mermaid. The woman whose effortless allure had hovered at the edge of his dreams all night, miraculously keeping far darker dreams at bay for the first time in weeks.

As she slid into full view her dark red curls streamed over her shoulders like waves of silk. Her pale skin was luminous in the weak morning light. The fine features of her face hid nothing. Not her loveliness, or her wariness. Again he wished he had his camera, on him. His camera which he had not picked up once in two long months.

'Well, hello there,' he said when she was near enough for him to see the whites of her guarded eyes.

'Hello,' she said, offering a half smile, even

though her clenched fists and ducked chin told him far more than the smile could hope to hide.

As did the black tank-top with a hot pink one beneath, the long hippy skirt and heavy black boots she'd run off in the day before. It would be close to thirty-five degrees later that day. Her feet must have felt like ovens. But he decided as soon as the thought occurred to him to keep that little titbit to himself. A wild bear she may not be, but there was an air of the intractable about her all the same.

'I didn't expect to see you here,' he said.

'I wasn't coming to use your pool, if that's what you mean.'

Hud laughed before he even felt it rising up his chest. It felt good. No, it felt great. Natural. Unforced. Curative. He held up both hands in surrender. 'Ah, no. I was just making conversation. Badly, it seems.'

She flicked her hair off her face. Not out of any kind of flirtation but more like she was shooing away a bothersome fly. Either way, the shift and tumble of her hair mesmerised him. The woman wasn't a mermaid, she was a siren. An unwilling siren, if that clenched jaw was anything to go by, but a siren all the same.

'You come here often?' he asked, wondering where these conversational gems were coming from.

'More often than I should probably admit,' she said with a shrug.

Hud didn't realise he had a thing for shoulders until that moment. Pale, delicate, eloquent shoulders were his new favourite thing.

'But I came out this morning in the hope I might bump into you,' she said as she finally made prolonged eye contact with him.

Well, that was one for the books. Hud stopped his daydreaming and came to attention. 'You could have come knocking on my front door,' he said. 'I think we've established you know where I live.'

Her eyes blazed and he bit his inner lip and told himself to cool it. The more he pushed, the more she seemed determined to pull away. But maybe it was worth it for the flare of energy in those blue-grey eyes.

'Not my style,' she said, the tight half smile shifting into something far more natural as it tugged at the corners of her lips. 'I tend to make things far more difficult than all that.'

'I've been there,' he said. And he smiled back, feeling it from the inside out.

Then her smile slid away and she shook her head and, with a big deep breath, said, 'Look, I wanted to apologise for yesterday. And all the days before that. The trespassing. The tidying. The water usage.' She closed one eye and squinted up at him through the other, obviously mortified at having to say so.

And it was just as obvious to him that he found this woman utterly adorable. Whoever she was. Whatever she was really here to say to him. Because he knew as well as he knew his own name that she sure wasn't here, hat in hand, just to say, *I'm sorry*.

'You have nothing to apologise for,' he said. 'The pool house never looked so good. Ever. I should have come looking for you at the other end of this forest of ours to say thank you.'

She opened the other eye and her eyebrows disappeared under wavy wisps of dark red hair. Her voice dropped when she said, 'It never looked that good *ever*? Maybe you should demand a refund from your previous pool guy.'

Hud laughed again. And his smile lingered. Grew, even. 'You needn't have worked nearly so hard at it.'

'How could I not? It's the most amazing structure I've ever seen. Like something out of a fairy tale.' She let go of a sigh. A long romantic sigh that seemed to curl about them both until Hud realised the sounds of the forest had slipped completely away until all he could hear was the sound of her voice, her breathing, the swish of her voluminous skirt.

Her eyebrows settled back to a normal position,

perhaps even a little furrowed as she shifted her stance as though her toes were turning numb in her shoes, and said, 'But, even so, you were no doubt surprised to find…what you found. And I feel utterly embarrassed. About the whole thing with the pool. Tidy though it is. And for thinking you were going to rob me. And for the running away without explaining myself.'

And? Hud thought. For she wasn't finished yet. He could almost see the wheels turning behind those smoky eyes. *Right,* she was thinking, *he's going to make me say this, isn't he?*

She squared her shoulders. Tossed her hair again. Looked him dead in the eye and said, 'But, since you think I've done such a good job of keeping your pool house in tiptop shape, perhaps we can come to some arrangement where I can continue.'

She tried to make it seem a *by the way* kind of statement, but he knew from the tightness in her neck and the way she grabbed hold of clumps of her tie-dyed skirt that this was what she'd come here to say.

Hud opened his mouth to tell her she could do whatever she liked, when she held up a hand, palm forward, and he stopped before the words made it past his larynx.

'I'm prepared to buy the chlorine, the tile cleaner, pay a portion of your water bill, get on my hands and knees and clean the grout with a toothbrush, anything. I just…' She stopped to swallow, and for the first time he saw a flutter of vulnerability beneath the resilient exterior. 'I just need to keep swimming in your pool. If it's okay with you.'

She made it seem as if she needed it the same way he needed oxygen in his lungs. The same way he needed to find out how to clear his head so that he could get back to work. And the way he had come out here into the misty forest with some strange need to make sure that she was real.

'Where on earth will you find the time to do all that?' he asked.

'I am a fact checker for several regional newspapers. I work freelance. My time management is my own.'

'Sounds pretty cushy.'

'Suits me. Not so many rave parties and shoe shops to keep a girl in trouble in Saffron, so one doesn't need a great deal of money to have a very nice life here.' She glanced over his shoulder to what was no doubt a gorgeous view of Claudel's elegant gabled rooftop beyond. 'Well, I don't, anyway.'

He didn't give her the satisfaction of turning. Instead he just waited for her pointed gaze to rock back to his. For suddenly he was having ideas.

Her time was her own. And he had nothing but time. Maybe this woman's needs and his could work together. He slid his hands into his pockets. 'So I take it you can type,' he said.

Her hands slowly let go of the skirt fabric they'd been clinging to until the red and black cotton swished about the tops of her heavy boots. 'Can I type?'

He nodded.

'So fast you won't see my fingers move for the speed. But I don't see what that has to do with—'

'I have a story I need to get down on paper,' he said. 'And I am a two-finger typist of the worst kind.'

'You're a writer? But I thought you were some kind of flashy documentary photographer,' she said, then her face dropped as she realised she'd given away the fact that she'd done some asking around about him.

'I am,' he said, letting her off the hook. 'But a situation has presented itself that means I need to record some of my more recent experiences.'

That much was true enough. He had been offered a book deal. A lucrative one from a big London publisher. Not that he needed the money. But if that was what it took for his boss to see he was willing and able to get back to work, to the ad-ventures he was missing out on while real life trudged on around him, then that was what he'd do.

'I see,' she said, mouth turned down, bottom lip popped out, nodding. Though by the look in her wide open eyes he could tell she couldn't see the brilliance of his plan at all. The balance. The simpatico.

'So I have a proposal for you,' he said.

She stopped nodding. Her eyes narrowed so far they became dark slits of mistrust. For a siren she was turning out to be some kind of hard work. Hud almost backed off. But not quite. For there was something stronger pushing between his shoulder blades again, telling him he had to go through with this. With her.

'I dictate,' he said. 'You type my story. And in return…'

Her arms slid across her chest to cross, creating a shield between them. He bit back the need to laugh. The woman was so guarded she put his clandestine return to Claudel to shame.

So he added, 'And in return you can use my pool as much as you like.'

She blinked furiously, then a fast breath dashed from her nose. 'What's the catch?'

'There's no catch. I'll supply food. A comfy chair. I can get my hands on a new computer if you need me to. It shouldn't take any longer than, say…two weeks.'

Which was when his crew were due back in London after a shoot in Uzbekistan. And he wanted to be on the next trip out. He *needed* to be. For, if he wasn't, he feared he might never get back out there again. And out there was where he belonged.

'Am I still in charge of its upkeep?' she asked.

He shook his head. 'No need. The whole place needs a tidy up. I'll have to hire a gardener. A backhoe. A mini-skip. Or maybe a magic wand to put things back the way they're meant to be.'

She nodded. 'Excellent. Happy with that. But what about after I've finished taking notes for you? What kind of deal will I have to make with you then?'

Her arms tightened across her chest, pressing her breasts together until she produced some damn fine cleavage. She glared at him and he tried his hardest to keep eye contact as her hot gaze dared him to even think that she might be thinking something raunchy. But the second the thought entered his mind he could think of little else.

A half hour swim for a kiss. An hour for a roll in the grass. A whole afternoon lazing in the pool and maybe she'd agree to going through the rest of Aunt Fay's rooms and deciding what furniture and knick-knacks to keep and which to let go. For that he'd let her have the darned pool.

'None,' he said. 'No more deals. Doing this one thing for me would be a huge favour, so for that you can use the pool any time you please. For evermore. So how about we clap hands and a bargain?' He held out his hand to seal the deal.

'*Henry V,*' she blurted, an honest-to-goodness smile creasing her lovely face. She was something when she frowned; she was something *else* again when she truly smiled. He decided then and there that if she agreed to his terms it would be his mission over the next two weeks to make that happen again and again.

Then her cheeks turned pink and she bit her lip and looked down at her right foot, which was kicking at a small pile of dead pine needles.

'Henry who or what?' Hud asked.

'*Clap hands and a bargain,*' she repeated, looking up at him from beneath her dark eyelashes. 'That was a quote from the proposal scene of *Henry V*. It'll make you laugh and cry and your heart go pitter-pat. And, if it doesn't, well then, I fear you're just not human.'

Hud took a moment to wet his suddenly dry throat. The woman not only had the hair of a Botticelli model, the skin of a Scandinavian princess and the ability to fill the dark nooks and crannies of his subconscious with light, but he had just accidentally stumbled upon a subject that made her eyes flash like the heralding of a summer storm.

When he said nothing she continued. 'Shakespeare. Dead English playwright. Quite famous in his time. Funny too that the line comes from the proposal scene and you just made me a proposal. Not like it's the same kind of proposal, of course. I'd hardly agree to marry a guy for the use of his amenities—'

'I have heard of him,' Hud said, cutting her off before she got herself so deep into a verbal hole that she disappeared into her shoes like the wicked witch at the end of *The Wizard of Oz*. 'Though I think it's too late to bluff my way into making you think I was quoting him on purpose. A guy I work with…used to work with, said it all the time. What's your excuse?'

'Double English Lit major at Uni,' she said, back to kicking at pine needles again as she breathed through her recent verbal misstep. 'That and a computer will get a girl a fine fact checking job with an added sideline in Shakespeare and Keats and Byron quotes on tap. I'm quite the hit at parties.'

'I don't doubt it for a second.' He'd be surprised if she ever made it out of a party without half a dozen new male fans. He wondered if one of those fans had managed to pin her down. Make her his. And if he truly knew what a gem he had. 'And might I say I'm suitably impressed. You're the first girl who has ever picked a Shakespeare quote when I've given one. Not that I'd rightly know.'

She grabbed a hunk of layered skirt and gave him a little curtsy. Yeah, it would be a fine thing if some guy at a party had taken this woman off the market. For though he was most enjoying looking, he hadn't come to Claudel to shop for that kind of…what? Tryst? Crush? Holiday romance? Stormy, once-in-a-lifetime, go-for-broke affair?

This girl was witty, cautious and beguiling. It had taken an instant for him to see she was the kind of woman a man could spend a lifetime unravelling, pleasing, knowing. But he didn't have a lifetime. He had two weeks. Which was more than he'd given any woman in years. He'd just have to be careful to remember that.

She flattened her skirt back to a less frivolous position. 'So who's the guy?' she asked.

Hud lifted his gaze from the fluttering movement of her pale hands to her magnificent eyes. He raised an eyebrow.

'Whose quotes you steal?' she continued. 'The guy with whom you used to work?'

'Ah. His name was Grant, a sound guy who works for Voyager Channel films.'

'His name…*was* Grant?' she asked, her voice suddenly softer, slower, winding itself around him like one of Aunt Fay's warm cashmere throw rugs.

'It still *is* Grant, actually. Will be for many long

years, I hope. He's fine. He's just a million miles away and I'm here, in the middle of backwoods Victoria, only it feels like he's gone when really that honour goes to me.'

When Hud stopped talking, his heart raced as if he'd climbed a mountain, when really all he'd done was tell this strange girl more than he'd told anyone about what he was really feeling. More than he'd told his boss. Or the doctors in London. Or the editor who'd thrown money at him to 'tell his tale'. Or any of the friends and colleagues who'd asked how he was every time they'd picked up the phone, which was more and more rare with every passing day.

'So do we have a deal?' he asked, knowing the time had come to bring this little rendezvous to a close. 'Your typing fingers for my pool?'

'Sure,' she said, her voice still soft, still making him feel as though she had somehow wrapped him in cotton wool.

This time she held out her hand to seal the deal. He stepped forward and took it, entering her personal space, that intangible area that contained a person's spent energy, and touched her for the very first time.

Her hand was small. Soft. Warm. Enveloped so wholly in his, it made him feel strong. Big. Commanding. It was a feeling he didn't realise until that moment had been lost somewhere over the past months. A feeling he wanted back. He wanted more. He *needed* more.

After a few seconds of simply holding hands, her stormy eyes darted to his. Blinking fast. Locking. Connecting. A current seemed to flow from her hand to his. Or maybe it was the other way around.

And in that moment he saw that she felt it too. This strange compulsion pulling them together. He saw in her eyes a deep-seated desire to hold on to him and not let go.

He understood his own reasoning completely. He was a man on the verge of drowning—in violent memories, in red tape, in commiserations where he was used to commendations. And she was a bright light. Sparky, warm, flitting just out of reach.

What a woman like her saw in a broken man in need of a shave, he had no idea. He had nothing to offer her bar his pool. He consoled himself with the knowledge that she seemed switched on. She'd figure it out soon enough.

He loosened his grip and let her go. She stretched out her fingers before clasping her hands behind her back.

'So when do we start?' she asked.

I'm afraid we already have, he thought. But all he said was, 'Tomorrow's fine with me. Unless you're busy.'

But she merely nodded. 'Mornings are always best for me. Projects tend to slide into my inbox around midday. So nine okay with you?'

'Sounds as good a time as any.'

She gave him a short wave and turned away, taking all that lovely vibrant energy with her.

'So why do you need this pool of mine so badly you're willing to give up your precious time for me?' he asked, not yet ready to see her go.

'Training for the Olympics,' she threw back.

'Then you'd better not forget your bathers,' he said.

She waved over her shoulder. 'Not for all the world.'

'Feel free to come through the front door next time.'

Her head turned, only slightly, but enough for him to see her smile. It was only half the wattage of the one from earlier but still his chest constricted in response.

'We haven't known one another all that long, Hud, but I think you already know me better than that.'

The way his name sounded on her tongue made it feel as if they'd known one another a thousand years, though it was the first time he'd ever heard it. And suddenly he realised he had no idea what her name was.

'Who *are* you?' he called out, knowing his interest went far beyond just knowing her name.

She turned to walk backwards, not in the least fearful that she'd walk into a tree. Perhaps she was a wood sprite, after all.

'The name's Kendall York,' she said. 'The first.' The half smile kicking up at one corner created a rosy cheek and a hollow cheekbone. Her bone structure was unbelievable. Photographable.

And, as she began to disappear back into the early morning shadows of the pine forest she seemed to know so well, she shot him one last smile and with it one last statement. 'If you'd simply asked nicely I would have helped type up your story for nothing, you know. I'm that kind of girl.'

The smile hit dead centre of his chest. Burrowing, melting, until it was too late to get a handle on it and pull it out. He said, 'And if you'd said no I still would have let you use my pool. I'm that kind of guy.'

Her steps faltered. Only slightly but enough for him to take a step forward, as though he'd be able to catch her if she fell, even though by now she was a good ten metres away.

'See you tomorrow, Hud,' was all she said.

'Looking forward to it, Kendall.'

And with that she picked up her pace and she and her heavy boots and hippy clothes walked away.

Hud watched her until she was no more than a sweet memory which he would happily allow to slide unbidden into his mind any time that day or night.

At a couple of minutes before nine the next morning Kendall stood at the Claudel edge of the pine forest.

A large hemp bag containing her laptop, the notebook she never went anywhere without and a red tartan pencil case she'd had since primary school weighed heavy on her shoulder. The plastic bag carrying her bathers and towel felt lighter than air.

She stared at the grey canted roof of Claudel's main house. And, as always when she stepped on these grounds, she closed her eyes and imagined herself surrounded by ladies in long white dresses and white hats playing croquet and gentlemen in linen suits drinking Long Island iced teas.

Her eyes flickered open and the view morphed into a garden on the verge of eating the house alive while she stood alone in one of her usual long layered skirts and heavy Doc Martens, rigid with the prospect of finding herself once again in the company of a man who made her feel…what?

Well, that was just it. He made her *feel*. Nervous. Clumsy. Funny. Feminine. With a flicker of those deep dark hazel eyes, a twitch of those sensuous lips, the rise and fall of that broad chest, he conjured feelings inside her she'd believed long since extinct.

And she'd been fine with them being extinct. For memories of a time when such feelings had been the centre of her life hadn't faded in the years since the boy who'd shared them with her had gone. Memories that had taught her that being emotionally open to someone made a person vulnerable to a thousand different kinds of hurt.

Not that she felt anything for this guy like she had for George. She barely remembered a time in her young life when George hadn't been there. The past three years without him she had felt as if she were walking through mist.

Two conversations with a stunning man did not a great love affair make, even for a girl who had studied romantic literature. But she still felt something. A flutter. A whisper. The beginning of something that could so easily turn into another thing. After having looked into Hud Bennington's eyes—twice—her nerves jangled at the very thought of coming face to face with him again.

She wanted that pool, she needed that pool, but had the deal she had made been the worse of two evils?

If she turned around now and broke their bargain surely she could find another way.

Another pool. There must be a hundred public pools this side of Melbourne. Where she would have to get into her bathers in front of people. People who would stare at her left leg, and point, and whisper and wonder.

Or what if she just went for a swim anyway? What could the guy really do? Call the police? Barricade the door? Set up a security barrier with lasers and cameras and snipers?

No. He'd asked for her help. Help she could all too easily give. She had the time, the skill and, beneath all of that, like a diamond-tough thread holding the whole deal together, she *wanted* to see him again. To know if the warm, delicious skittery feeling enveloping her as she'd fallen asleep the night before had as much to do with him as she thought it had.

Well, stuff it. She'd had a crush on Lord Byron when she was twelve and she'd survived it. Now she was three times the age and had learnt the value of self-control. So long as the flutter of her heart didn't interfere with access to the pool, she could certainly appear all business. All the way.

She sucked in a long breath, allowing the clean scent of the forest to give her strength, and she strode up to the side door of the house. Her hand shook only slightly when she lifted it to rap on the big carved wooden door.

'Good morning,' a deep voice said from somewhere behind her.

Kendall spun to find Hud walking towards her, naked from the waist up. Well-worn jeans clung to his hips. Heavy boots caked in mud balanced out his impossibly broad shoulders. And, using his T-shirt as a pouch, he carried a pile of potatoes, tomatoes and carrots which he must have found in a vegetable garden that had survived the years.

The nearer he came, the harder she found it to swallow. Her neck suddenly felt warm and prickly. For it had been some time since she'd been this close to a wall of male muscle. If ever. George had been academic. A smart guy with the softest lips on the planet. But when his life had been snuffed with the slightest swerve of a steering wheel, he'd been a kid compared with the man who stood before her now.

She blinked rapidly, suppressing those memories and thoughts deep down inside.

Hud lifted his right arm to wipe it across his brow and Kendall caught sight of a tattoo etched on to his upper arm, spanning his large bicep. It was a word. A name. A woman's name. *Mirabella*.

She nibbled at her bottom lip.

Was she some ex-girlfriend? Or maybe even a current one? Hud's wife, even? An intrepid journalist still on the trail? Or a native of some far-flung exotic location who'd stolen his heart for ever, making it wretchedly untouchable.

His arm dropped and she glanced up to find him watching her with one of those faint half smiles that made her stomach tumble.

'Busy morning?' She dropped her hand to the strap biting at her shoulder and hitched it to a more comfortable position.

He shrugged and the half smile unexpectedly grew a matching blush, which on a guy of his size just made her feel all gooey inside. 'Sorry about my state of undress. I'm still on London time. I've been up with the birds. I had no idea what time it was.'

'I guess that means we're even,' she said. And then regretted bringing up the whole *I was there without permission and naked bar my swimmers* thing again when she saw understanding dawn. Understanding and a further darkening of his already unfairly dark eyes.

'So we are,' he said. 'So have you been for a swim yet?'

'Not yet. I thought I ought to work before claiming my prize. I have no intention of taking any further advantage of you…I mean, of your pool.'

'Don't worry about it. Swim in the mornings if it suits. Especially with the Olympics just around the corner and all.'

She felt her cheeks loosen and warm. She bit

back a smile as she said, 'I was pulling your leg about that.'

'No. Really?' Sarcasm dripped from his words and the smile spilled across her lips anyway.

'Yes, really. I need the pool because I'm secretly a synchronised swimming choreographer by trade. I just don't want it to get out or I'll have people beating on my door.'

'Right. Makes perfect sense.'

After a few long, loaded seconds in which the scent of pine needles and late roses mixed with the scent of warm male skin, Hud continued towards her. Kendall swayed back on to her heels.

He reached out to her at the last second. She felt all of her promises to brush off her infatuation melting away with the encroaching heat of day. Of him. Her breath clutched against the edges of her throat.

His hand caressed her shoulder, slid deftly beneath the strap of the too heavy bag, lifted it away from her grasp as though it weighed no more than a handful of feathers. And then he passed, bathing her in a whisper of sandalwood scent, pausing only slightly to throw a quick, 'Coming?' over his shoulder before disappearing into the belly of the house.

And if Kendall ever wanted to see her laptop again she had no choice but to follow.

As to finding an opportunity to discover who this Mirabella might be, well, she would just have to remind herself on a minute by minute basis why that was just none of her business.

CHAPTER THREE

THE neat elegance of the outside of the house had given Kendall little indication of the grandeur inside Claudel's high walls.

Cream wallpaper embossed with pale gold roses drew her through the side hall and into a massive parlour where oak floors were inset with marble friezes in the shape of more roses. The ceiling there was so high she had to crane her neck to see up into the second level, which was bordered with a gallery all the way around. Through arched doorways she spotted hallways leading to rooms and wings in every direction with hints of curling staircases winding up into hidden alcoves. It was huge. Beautiful. Graceful. Like something out of an art history book.

But for all that she detected not an ounce of warmth. Every piece of furniture was covered in white sheets as though the house was closed up and the family still away. Hud's return had not let any new air into the place.

'Kendall,' a dismembered voice said from somewhere to her right. She walked gently so that her clodhopper boots didn't echo through the lofty entrance.

She soon found Hud in a large room, backlit by bolts of light angling through several arched windows with their gold velvet curtains drawn back. Thankfully he'd added a clean T-shirt to his ensemble. If she'd had to sit there with him shirtless she wasn't quite sure she'd get through the morning without bursting a blood vessel or two.

She spied her hemp laptop bag at Hud's feet just before he blocked her view by whipping a large white sheet from a piece of furniture between them. Great swathes of dust came away with the fabric, bathing him in a hazy golden light, haloing his dark curls.

'No need for all this fanfare,' she said, then cleared her throat when her voice came out a tad ragged, which had nothing to do with the dust. 'I'm used to much more simple conditions. I usually work at a second-hand Formica desk beside the kitchen. Or, if Taffy kicks me off the big computer, then with my laptop on my lap in front of the TV.'

Hud curled the sheet into a ball and placed it beside a couch that looked as if it had only just been brought back out into the sunlight for the first time in years itself.

'That table is second-hand too, you know,' he said, turning suddenly to face her and catching her staring.

Kendall quickly dragged her eyes away from his and to the table to which he was referring. Bevelled edges, Queen Anne legs, antique as all get out. She looked back at him with a raised eyebrow. 'I'd hazard a guess my Formica number was never named after, and certainly never *owned* by, royalty.'

'You probably have me there.' He watched her for a further few seconds, a gentle smile warming his face. She gave into a sudden need to breathe deep.

Then, easy as you please, he turned away and she rocked back on to her heels as though he'd had his finger curled into the front of her tank-top and had finally let her go.

Kendall plonked on to the velvet-backed chair behind the makeshift desk, knees together, back ramrod straight, still holding on to her swimming bag, not quite sure what she was expected to do while he set to, pulling more sheets off all the furniture in the room. It did look more welcoming when he was done, and made her feel less like they were little kids trespassing. One less tension to worry about.

Eventually Hud stood surveying the room, hands on hips, chest pushed forward, dark eyes flickering over every detail like a soldier casing an enemy camp. 'So, this Taffy…' he said, catching her unawares. 'That can't be little Taffy Henderson, can it?'

She blinked and let her pool bag drop to the polished wood floor at her feet with a swoosh. 'Ah, yeah. Though she's not so little any more.'

He shook his head. 'I was sure she would have been living in New York by now, treading the Broadway stage. She was always a little drama queen.'

Kendall laughed out loud despite herself. 'Ah, no. She is the receptionist for the local accountants.' After a pause she added, 'She saves the drama queen antics for when she's at home.'

His gaze swung sideways to engage hers. A matching smile lit his eyes. Her stomach lurched, skidded and fell over backwards with a splat she felt reverberate through her whole body.

'Lucky you,' he said.

'You have no idea.'

'So she's your…' He let the thought carry on the air between them.

'Friend. I rent a room in her house. We've known one another since we were in high school together. She was a couple of years above me. The rest is a long story.'

'I have nothing but time,' he said, ambling towards her.

Her head tilted higher the nearer he came. He was backlit, the hard planes of his face in shadow. And once again she felt a warning thump in the back of her head. Only now she knew it had nothing to do with the fear that came from being alone with a stranger in a secluded place. It came from finding herself alone with him.

'I used to date her cousin,' she said, so distracted she didn't even feel the words until they spilled from her mouth.

Hud's brow furrowed. 'Another local? Would I know him?'

'No,' Kendall said, running a hand up the back of her neck to negate the sudden tightness constricting her muscles. 'We all went to school in Melbourne. Taffy stayed with George's family during the week and his family lived near mine. Anyway, I have about half a dozen articles due back at the paper by three, and a swim to fit in between, so…'

'Of course,' he said. 'Sorry. I'd completely forgotten that's the reason you're here.'

She slid her battered old laptop from its case and with it her ubiquitous red notebook. She turned on her laptop, balanced her fingers over the keys, half the letters long since worn away, and purposely didn't look at Hud any more.

But, after several drawn-out moments, she

couldn't help herself. Something about this place seemed to have her checking her will-power at the border of the pine forest.

She looked up to find Hud standing in the middle of the room, one hand on his hip, the other running up the back of his neck in a mirror image of her recent action, as though something heavy was bothering him too. His bicep strained against the cotton of his T-shirt, pale denim hung just so off lean hips, and he looked at her. Worse, he looked *into* her.

As though the well-built, well-tended, protective walls that normally kept her safe from a return of any kind of emotional disorder into her life were to him as transparent as cellophane. As though he knew the half a dozen articles she had due back to *The Northern News* weren't the reason why she wanted to get on with their deal and quick.

She was here because she was drawn to him. But whether it was to his sad eyes or his beautiful face she had no idea. Either ought to have kept her strapped to her desk at home instead of sitting here becoming more and more familiar with every tempting facet, for both were so enticing she wasn't sure quite how to escape their pull.

She let her wrists slump against the table and the breath she let go was juddery and hot, as if it had been pent up inside her for an eternity. Her skin began to itch as if a rash were crawling up her arm, as she waited for him to say something, to tell her what he saw. And her head spun as she tried to think of ways to *not* answer him.

'So,' he said, his hand dropping until his long arm rested at his side, 'if you're comfortable there, I'm happier to walk as I talk. Okay with you?'

Kendall licked her dry lips. She would have been more comfy on the couch by far, feet on the coffee table, laptop warming her thighs, but that would have put her nearer Hud and his sandal-wood scent and that would have been tantamount to giving the guy the sledgehammer to knock down her walls for good.

'Fine with me,' she said.

'Right,' he said. 'Then let's go ahead and get this thing done.'

This thing, Hud repeated in his head. As if getting the story of the last two months of his life out of his head and down on paper was some kind of distraction getting in the way of other things the two of them could be doing together.

But *this thing* was the reason he was here. While *she* was the distraction. No doubt about it. All that dewy skin and those great big eyes and complex personality were enough to keep a guy like him—a guy with an infamously short attention span—interested.

Over the years he'd found women the world over who were happy to be distractions to a man who wore his inherent resistance to settling in one place like a second skin. Somehow, more often than not, they sought him out rather than the other way around. As though a friendly ear and a warm pair of arms could get many an aimless soul through the night.

But he knew instinctively that this woman was not like the others. She wouldn't take being a distraction lightly. Giving into such urges would only be taking advantage. Which he had to tell himself over and over again while she sat there, looking up at him expectantly, eyes dark against her pale skin, believing she was part of something bigger than just the slaying of the monsters inside of his head.

He began to pace. Trying to find a beginning point, a way in. For now he actually had to say the words out loud to begin to get *this thing*—this great, dark, hulking shadow hovering over his future like a storm cloud waiting to burst—out of him and through her. Not his most brilliant scheme ever, though when an excess of hormones became involved most men could be said to be less than at their prime.

Kendall slowly sucked her lips between her teeth and her hands fell to cradle the edges of her laptop. '*Once upon a time* is a tad clichéd,' she said. '*I was born* has already been taken. But anything else would suffice.'

'Thanks,' he said, shooting her a wry smile. And deciding that perhaps the walking thing wasn't helping. He sat on the couch, grabbed a velvet throw pillow, punched it a few times and tucked it into a corner of the couch before lying down and using it as a pillow. But then he felt far too much like he was on a psychiatrist's couch.

He sat up, clasped his hands so tight around his kneecaps his knuckles turned white and figured he may as well start the day it happened.

'Colombia,' he said, the word shooting from his lungs as though it had to pass through an obstacle course. He closed his eyes and breathed through it, doing his all to control the images already starting to crowd in on him.

Bad idea. Bad idea, his subconscious chanted. Then, *Just be a man, and do it*.

He looked across and noticed that, while Kendall's right leg was stretched out comfortably in front of her, she was kneading her left thigh. Her expression was absent-minded, her brow furrowed.

'You okay?' he asked, happy for the interruption.

She looked up. He motioned to her leg.

And then, quick as a flash, she straightened her skirt, a twin to the one from the day before, only this one was the colour of caramel, then folded both legs back beneath her. 'All good,' she said with an easy smile. 'Keep going. So far it's riveting. I can only hope the rest can live up to the promise so far.'

'Smart alec,' he said, but what he thought was, *Be careful what you wish for...*

'Night,' he continued. 'A sky of dark blue. Market umbrellas like triangular black holes against the squat, square mud buildings surrounding the town centre. Their dark windows like empty eyes looking out over the noisy milling crowd. I pass a group of young men leaning against a building, smoking, laughing, telling dirty jokes.'

When he paused to finally take a breath, he didn't hear any typing. He glanced across to find Kendall with her chin resting on her palm, just watching him. Her smoky eyes had fuzzed over as if she were caught up in his story. But he knew there was no story as yet, just window-dressing. Which could only mean she had been caught up in...

She cleared her throat loudly and came to, her cheeks turning pink. 'Sorry, I take it we've begun?'

He laughed through his nose, releasing a measure of the tension building inside him. For a closet distraction, she worked wonders. Little in the world surprised him after a decade of photographing things he half hoped most people would go a lifetime without seeing, yet this creature continued to do so.

She was the unexpectedness of a summer shower, the energy of a bolt of sunshine and the precariousness of fork lightning all rolled into one. And, for someone who spent half her time glowering at him as if she thought he might still only be at Claudel to steal the silver, there were definite moments when he was sure she was thinking far more inventive thoughts about him.

'Yes, we've begun,' he said.

'Excellent news.' Her tongue slid across her bottom lip, leaving behind a pink sheen that he could quite happily stare at for hours.

'Colombia. Empty eyes. Dirty jokes,' she said as she typed from memory. Then her pale brow furrowed and she looked up, wide eyes concerned. 'What kind of book is this, exactly? Just so I know what kind of layout, tense, structure, font, line-spacing and grammar I ought to be using from the outset. No point in double handling.'

'It's not exactly a book per se. It's more of a…' *A job obligation? A self-indulgence? A waste of time? An exorcism?* 'More of a memoir.'

'A *memoir*? A little young to be going down that route, don't you think? And a little less of a movie star or renowned politician to warrant such a thing? I mean, no offence, but seriously?'

Hud uncurled his fingers from the death grip on his knees, leant back against the sofa and reached out both arms along the back, a good portion of his strain easing out through his extended fingertips as his focus turned one hundred per cent to Kendall's eyes, which were lively with deliciously grounding scepticism.

In that moment he truly felt as if nothing really bad could happen in the company of someone like her, in such a lovely setting. God let things slide the world over, but he wouldn't be so cruel as to dampen such pretty eyes. Surely.

'Stick around,' he said, his voice dropping, sliding all too easily from tension to flirtation, 'and you'll soon find out.'

She blinked at his playful tone. All gorgeous dark eyelashes and splendidly prickly overtones. She was quite simply the most captivating creature he'd happened upon in a very, very long time.

'Fair enough. Shall do,' she said, then poised her fingers back atop the keys, with a look in her eye as though she was preparing herself to be blinded by something a good deal less than brilliant. 'Go right ahead. Memoir away.'

He crossed his foot atop the other knee. 'What was I up to?'

'Smoking, laughing, telling dirty jokes. And then…'

And then…

He didn't want to do this. He wasn't in the mood to walk down that dark alley again. And he wasn't all that thrilled about taking this woman there with him. Not when he honestly preferred it when she looked at him with inventive thoughts behind her eyes.

He stood. And, spying the pile of rolled up drop cloths on the floor, he said, 'How do you feel about cataloguing my aunt's furniture instead? I have no idea where to even start.'

He glanced up, hoping she'd shrug and say *sure*. But her mouth hung open like a kid who'd just been told there would be no Christmas this year.

'No? You seemed pretty interested in the history of that table earlier. I am sure there are documents somewhere in this big old place telling you all about them. Think of all the lovely factoids you can add to your repertoire.'

She swallowed and then said, 'I was kind of hoping you might give me some kind of acknowledgement in your…memoir; it could help me get this kind of gig again. Ghost-writing even.'

'You'd like to be a writer? As well as a fact checker and synchronised swimming choreographer?'

She smiled, her cheeks turning a lovely shade of pink that clashed beautifully with her dark red hair. 'Aah, that was a bit of a fib as well, I'm afraid.'

'I'm shocked. So why the love of my pool?'

'Electrolytes,' she shot back so fast he almost believed her this time.

'Electrolytes,' he repeated.

'Mmm-hmm. I saw something on a current affairs show a couple of years back. A daily swim keeps your electrolytes balanced and the proper amount and distribution in the body is essential for good health.'

'Of course it is.' Hud laughed, the sensation grabbing him by the middle and shaking all sorts of things loose. Until he felt lax and lazy, as if he could sit in that room and talk to this woman until the world outside turned dark. 'I can see you're an accomplished story teller already, Ms York. It wouldn't be such a big leap to try to make a profession of writing fiction.'

'I couldn't hope to write fiction. I read too much at University to know when I'm beat. But I like to collect events, I guess.' She reached out, her hand hovering over a red hardback notebook. 'Since I was a kid I've written down funny lines from TV shows. Old movies that touched me. Songs I want to download. Places that have stuck with me. Moments that have special resonance.

People who've made an impression. Memories I can feel beginning to fade. Kind of like a travelogue of a life rather than a place.'

She flicked a quick glance his way, her eyes narrowing sharply when she seemed to remember to whom she was giving all these insights into her imagination. He only wondered if he'd made enough of an impression to make it into the pages of her precious notebook, and how much he'd like to get a glimpse of what she had to say about him if he had.

'Sounds like you should be writing editorials. Have you run it by any of the papers you work for?' he asked.

'Oh, God, no. Nobody would be interested in reading about my dreary existence. It's just one of those private dreams all girls have, like wanting to be a pop star or a princess. Silly, really.' She brought her hands to her face to cool her suddenly pink cheeks. 'It's not like I've ever actually said anything out loud about it before. To anybody. Just forget I said anything.'

She shook her head in seeming amazement that she'd said the words out loud to *him*. Had shared her secret dreams. And there he was, swallowing down his secret nightmares. She thought herself lacking in courage? Well, that didn't say a great deal about him.

And that was the problem. He could feel that way for evermore if he didn't deal with it now. The last thing he wanted was to be hiding out in some Thai marsh and suddenly find himself in the middle of a debilitating flashback.

He pinched the soft skin between his left thumb and forefinger. 'Maybe we could do a little more writing, then. So you can see how you go making a travelogue of someone else's life.'

She swallowed then, her long pale throat working hard. 'Sure. If you're still okay with that, I'm in. Share away.'

He turned his back and stared blankly towards the large bay windows looking out over the front of the house, knowing well enough that her sweet face would only make him put on the brakes.

'We were there doing a story on the rise of Colombian coffee,' he said, 'by way of small family holdings. We had retired to the nearby town of Salento. Had dinner. A few drinks with the locals, who were getting to know us after three weeks camped out there. It was dark, but not late. I was ready to retire, leaving the others to drink out the night. I remember the compacted dirt footpath at my feet looked like patches of pooled gold beneath the triple torch lights as I turned towards the hotel.'

'Poetic,' Kendall said and he looked over his shoulder to find her finally typing away happily.

He turned fully, drawn despite himself to watch her instead of blank space filled only with images of approaching violence. 'I'm a photographer. The visuals are what stay with me. Ask me what song was playing on the radio when I woke up this morning…I wouldn't have a clue. What I ate for dinner last night, I'd have to think long and hard. But ask me what colour skirt you wore yesterday in the pine forest, the pattern on your towel in the pool house, or the exact colour of your eyes and I would not get it wrong.'

The keyboard went silent, just as he'd known it would. He could almost hear the wheels in her head turning from interest in his story to interest in something far more immediate. She didn't look at him, keeping her lowered eyes firmly on the laptop screen. But her chest rose and fell as she took heavy breaths.

After several long moments her eyes fluttered closed. Her voice was strong, challenging even, as she said, 'Go on, then.'

'Blue,' he said, without hesitation. 'In this kind of untempered sunlight they are blue. In the shadows of the forest they are far more grey. And in the pool house, in that odd half light, with shadows and sunbeams and reflections of both, they are just like the sky before a thunderstorm.'

Her eyes flickered back open, lifted and clashed

with his, dark and fuelled by a heady mix of temptation and denial. Hud realised his breaths were
coming heavier than they ought as well.

He wondered if he could go so far as telling her
that they were the most extraordinary eyes he'd
ever seen. Rich with emotion, glinting with energy
and so wide open that every time he looked into
them he found it harder and harder to look away.

Before he had the chance to fall into such a
deep, dangerous black hole, she looked away first,
tilting her head so that she could scratch a hand
through her hair.

'Nice party trick,' she said, her voice cooler
than her still pink cheeks. 'I can make my big
toes creak, which always goes down a treat. So,
where were we?'

Her eyes flittered over the screen, as though
she couldn't see the words right before her nose.
She scrunched her hands into fists and then
opened them out flat.

'Pools of gold,' Hud said. Though all he could
visualise was the fierce beauty of the several great
thunderstorms he had survived in his time, and
whether putting his arms over his head and his
fingers in his ears and running for cover could
save him from the one he felt coming.

CHAPTER FOUR

'Are you a coffee drinker?' Hud asked.

Kendall's brow furrowed at the sudden change of subject. In fact she was finding it difficult to keep up at all. She'd written all of two hundred words, and she still had no real idea what about. Her cheeks felt unnaturally hot, her fingers cramped and her breath laboured. Which, for an endeavour that was meant to be all business, was just crazy.

'I…excuse me?' she said.

'Coffee. For the sake of argument. Would you know a good coffee from a bad? A Colombian from a Kenyan?'

'I'm afraid I'm not the one you need to be asking. I've drunk instant coffee with milk and sugar my whole life and as far as I know it comes from a glass jar.'

'Until Colombia I was the same, always drank what I'd been given.'

'What about Colombia changed you?'

His smile shifted, and grew, and his tongue darted out to rest on his bottom lip as he ran a finger over his chin, and she wondered what she'd said that was so funny.

'Sitting down with the Salinas family at a rustic wooden table built five generations earlier, drinking coffee grown and roasted on the premises was one thing. But when you consider they work against the backdrop of daunting transportation problems and the constant threat of social and political conflict, their coffee tastes like nothing else on earth. Sweet, syrupy and intense. Promise me you'll one day try Colombian, from the Valle del Cauca if at all possible.'

Kendall wasn't typing. Wasn't even remembering she was meant to be. She was just resting her chin on her upturned palm and watching him talk about faraway happenings in faraway places.

When she didn't say anything for a while, he turned to face her, his dark hazel gaze, the colour of which she too could recite, down to the gold flecks in the left and the darker ring around the right, resting easily upon hers.

'Promise?' he asked.

She nodded, not even remembering his original question but pretty much ready to promise him any darned thing he wanted. 'I promise.'

He nodded right on back and Kendall had to remind herself to breathe out.

'So do you pick your stories and your locations?'

'Nope. I go where Voyager sends me. They link the crew with the photographer, and the crew with the subject matter. I never know until about a week before where I'm going.'

'Isn't that kind of scary, having your life so far out of your control?'

'Nah. Control is overrated. Or an illusion at best. Once you accept that life is a game of chance it makes everything else far less complicated.'

That was the first hint of blatant cynicism she'd heard from his lips. It had hovered around him like a dark cloud since that first day, but her initial instinct was confirmed in that moment.

Hud Bennington was restless. Scrappy. A high risk prospect. The exact opposite of the forces Kendall had purposely surrounded herself with since her life had spun so thoroughly out of her control on a dry, straight stretch of road three years earlier.

'I'm afraid I'm quite the opposite,' she said. 'I can't even leave the house without a list of things that need doing that day.'

'I tell you, by letting go of expectations and necessities I've seen more of the world than most people could hope to see in ten lifetimes.'

Escapades and adventures had been the order of the day when she was in her teens. She'd been a free spirit then. Precocious and breezy to George's earnestness. A bit of a wild child with no mother and an emotionally absent father.

But now expectations, necessities, control, routine, comfort and sameness were the order of the day. Such a life lacked the high highs, but it absolutely made up for it in its lack of low lows. Which was just as she wanted it to be.

Why then had she trespassed, secretly kept Hud's pool to herself, and now agreed to this crazy deal despite the tumble of warm and singular feelings he created inside her? She was living so far outside the boundaries of her safe routine it should have been terrifying. But instead his words were blinking frantically in her mind like some kind of enticing Las Vegas casino sign.

'I can't believe I actually feel envious of you,' she admitted. 'To simply get up and go and *not* look back. I can't even imagine how freeing that must be. I constantly have one eye on the ground at my feet so I don't trip over and another over my shoulder so as not to repeat the mistakes of my past.'

Kendall's completely unexpected and honest acknowledgement made Hud feel much more of a fraud. As if he were playing the part of Hudson Bennington III, voracious adventure-junkie, when if all that was true he'd be back out there right now. No qualms.

'I've *always* wanted to travel,' she continued.

He took a deep breath before saying, 'So travel. It's as easy as packing a bag and hopping on a jet plane. Or getting in a car and picking a road and driving until you hit an ocean somewhere.'

'Don't have a passport. Don't have a car.' She dropped her elbow from the table and her hands clasped in her lap, her shoulders slumping. 'I haven't been further north than here or further south than Melbourne my whole life.'

Hud blinked. Floored by her all over again. 'How does that happen to a…how old are you?'

Her eyes shot to his. Defensive. 'Twenty-three. How old are you?'

That stopped him cold. At thirty-two he could almost be classed a different generation. 'Let's just say I'm older.'

He vaguely remembered twenty-three as being a time when he'd been most fearless. Yet this woman was *dreaming* of travel, making moon eyes at a man almost ten years her senior, rather than being out there in the big wide world meeting someone more appropriate. And available. And he was a selfish bastard in encouraging her.

'So get a passport,' he said, cooling his voice, and his enthusiasm. 'Get a car.'

He saw the moment she felt the freeze. She sat up straighter and even took the time to lean back in her chair and cross her arms before glaring at him.

Good, he thought, *much better*.

'Funds also help,' she said, her voice equally cool.

'That they do. Though desire matters far more than anything else.'

'Desire?'

The way the word sparked off her tongue made it seem far more potent than he'd meant in that context.

'A desire to know the world,' he explained, his voice a deep rumble.

In response her eyes grew just a touch wider, her pupils just a touch darker, and his solar plexus clenched hard.

'Next you're going to tell me if I wish hard enough and dream long enough anything's possible,' she said.

'Maybe it is.' Then, like a slide show of photographs flipping before his eyes, he visualised taking her to London, to Shakespeare's revamped Globe, to his favourite hotel in Paris with its barely there view of the top of Notre Dame, to the ruins of Machu Pichu. And watching her emotions spill across her face as she found the village in Namibia where it took as little as every member of his crew to donate a week's pay to send thirty local children to school for a year.

He dragged himself back to the present and gave himself a good mental shake. This conversation was about the dreams of a small town girl, not the self-seeking fantasies of a world-weary traveller.

'Make yourself do it one day. You'll discover the world doesn't revolve around Saffron, or you. It's actually kind of liberating, you know.' Okay, so he was being a prick. But better that than the object of her admiration.

'You think I feel like the world revolves around me?'

'Don't you? I sure did when I was your age.'

Her face lost a touch of colour. He bit the inside of his cheek to numb the discomfort it caused in his gut.

'Well, no. As a matter of fact, I do not.'

'Don't your problems feel bigger than everyone else's? Your mistakes more far-reaching? Isn't that what makes you need to look over your shoulder all the time?'

The air around him suddenly felt thick and heavy. And cold. Hard as it was to believe one single woman could change the temperature in a room, if anyone had such supernatural powers this extraordinary woman would be the one.

'You can't even presume to think you know me,' she said, her voice reed-thin. 'Or my problems.'

He held up his hands in surrender but, by the storm that had long since arrived in her eyes, he knew it was too late.

Kendall tried to control her breathing, but her anger had gone past all that. This guy was tying her in complete knots. One second she found herself melting under his hot gaze, the next he may as well have been yawning he seemed so ambivalent towards her.

She wanted to shake him, and then shake herself for good measure. But that would mean standing on legs that felt as if they had been swept out from under her. So the only weapon left in her arsenal was verbal.

'Tell me this, Hud,' she said. 'You're some kind of gazillionaire, right?'

Hud leant his chin on his palm and rubbed a finger back and forth along his jaw. Kendall could easily have been hypnotised by the action drawing her attention to the cut of his beautiful chin. But the expression in his eyes as he pondered her question was as though she'd asked him his favourite colour, and that made it easy enough to keep right on feeling angry.

'Well,' she continued, 'with such an immodest name as yours, either you come from money or your mother was seriously hopeful. And, so far as gossip lets on, this house is all yours. Not yours and the Saffron branch of the National Bank. Just yours.'

His finger kept up its easy pace. Left, right. Sliding beneath his lower lip and then back again, leaving his swarthy jaw open for inspection. 'It is.'

'So I'm thinking it's not all that stands between you and your next buttered toast or you'd have sold it off for a lump of easy cash years ago when it was left to you.'

'I don't need to sell Claudel in order to eat, no.'

'I, on the other hand, live pay cheque to pay cheque, which is only one of myriad reasons why desire alone hasn't been enough to get me on a plane and out of here. While you walk around with this *I am small and insignificant just like you despite my quazillions* act you've got going on. Is that why you dress like such a bum? So the rest of us don't slap you silly for having the gall to tell us how the world turns?'

His finger finally stopped moving, and Kendall blinked to get her focus back. Lost in the mist of an unexpectedly vociferous reaction, she'd gone too far. She hardly knew this guy. Oh, hell, she was going to have to apologise again, wasn't she?

But then Hud laughed. So loud and so hard that he threw his head back and she was witness to musculature working in a long tanned throat and

more stubble than she quite knew how to cope
with. A wave of undiluted attraction swept
through her. Red. Hot. Invigorating. Shooting way
past the edges of her carefully controlled emotional register.

She crossed her arms again, locked her knees
together and wiggled her toes so that she could
hurry up and get up and get out of here without
shaking or, far worse, limping.

Hud's laughter died down to a smile. The smile
of a guy in an aftershave commercial. A self-made
man. With latent power flowing like a trapped
current beneath his skin. The kind of guy who
liked playing pool and drinking beer and telling
tall tales with his mates, yet who could tango a
woman across any dance floor in the world and
straight into bed without breaking a sweat.

'Did you really just say I look like a bum?' he
asked.

'You do,' she shot back, pinching her upper
arms to keep herself grounded. 'Your jeans look
older than this house. Your T-shirts have holes in
them. And your watch face is so scratched you can
barely see the time in it.'

'What would you prefer I wear?' he asked with
a smile in his deep voice.

Kendall uncrossed her arms and glanced
down at her hands, which were shaking a tiny

little bit. This conversation wasn't going as she'd meant it to.

'If you're angling for a lift into Melbourne to hit the shops,' Hud said, 'just ask. If Fay's Bentley is still around, then we have a car at our disposal.'

We? *We?* 'No, I'm…that's not what I was trying to say. It's just, I've never known a guy who seems to not care, about anything, as much as you do. Or don't. Or whichever is grammatically correct.'

'So says the English major.'

'English lit, thank you very much. And they had some crazy grammar in Elizabethan times.'

Hud laughed again and Kendall felt it rolling across her skin, over her shoulders, loosening everything inside and out. If only he was local, and less gorgeous, and more down-to-earth, and less a hero out of an old action movie, and more settled, then maybe, maybe she could truly allow herself to trip and tumble as readily as her feet and heart were willing her to do.

'I care about plenty of things, Kendall. Perhaps just not the same things you do.'

'Like what?' she asked.

'Is this for the book?' he asked, his brow furrowing.

'No,' she said, realising it had been some time since she'd thought about the book. 'This is just for me.'

He nodded, the small smile lingering at the

corners of his beautiful mouth. He shifted on the sofa until both feet hit the ground, his elbows rested on his knees and his hands formed a steeple. 'Packing light,' he began, 'wet weather protection for my camera, comfort in extreme temperatures, language barriers, unstable governments and time and again accidentally finding at the other end of a lens images so lamentable they'd break a giant's heart.'

Kendall swallowed, blind-sided. She'd been trying to accuse him of being lazy and cynical when all the while he had the sensitive soul of an artist. Could he possibly be any more enticing?

'Well, that kinda makes my fashion statement seem a little superficial,' she said. 'And, in connection, me.'

He glanced her way and for a second she wondered if he'd even remembered she was in the room. He wasn't tying her in knots. She was doing a fine job of it all on her own.

'Hud, I think from now on we can agree to stick to the original rules of the deal. You talk, I type, then I swim, and we do it all again tomorrow.'

Hud's gaze finally focused on her eyes, pinning her to the back of the chair with his intensity. She felt as if her temperature had raised a good degree.

'Miss York,' he said, 'that sounds like the most sensible thing I've heard all day.'

* * *

Hud talked shop like a good boy. He told Kendall how he'd sold his first photo to *The Northern News*, a paper for which she now worked. How he'd been the youngest ever photographer to land an exclusive gig with Voyager Enterprises. And about the untroubled beginnings of the trip to the Valle del Cauca in Colombia.

While she finished typing a sentence he watched as she bit at her luscious bottom lip. It was one of several fascinating tics he'd chanced upon. Others he liked were the double vertical furrow between her brows when she struggled to type fast enough. The small happy sigh when they hit the end of a scene. But it was the constant nibbling of her lip that had him wondering how so many of his sentences had come out more intelligible than, *Ugh*.

Intelligible, sure. But certainly not the kind of thing anybody would pay thirty bucks to read, or half a million to publish as one British firm had offered while he had been lying in a hospital bed with a drip in his arm.

Several times she'd stopped typing to simply look at him, studying his face as though she could tell he was avoiding something. He wondered if she outright demanded he cut the bull, whether he would still be able to hold back. Whether the siren call of those great emotive eyes of hers would be too much for him to deny.

After two solid hours Kendall stretched out her fingers. 'So you speak fluent Spanish?'

'That I do. And a smattering of French. Russian. Pretty good Italian. Enough to get me by in most places.'

'That's impressive.'

'Not as impressive as speaking Shakespearean. I was always ninety-nine per cent certain that stuff was just gibberish.'

'No,' she said, the double brow furrow very much in place. 'You can't believe that.'

'I can and I do. All that alas and alack stuff just rattled inside my head when I studied it in high school.'

Her eyes lit bright with passion. 'But it's so worth discovering. Take your time. Listen to the flow and feel of the words. Don't try too hard and it'll just come to you. Glorious and textured and funny and moving and fabulous. I'll try Colombian coffee if you promise me you'll give Will another go.'

He smiled. 'I promise.'

'Excellent. Now my turn: when do I get to see some pictures to go with these words of yours?'

'Pictures?'

'Your photos. Surely this will be a pictorial memoir as well.'

'Yeah,' he said, 'of course.'

'Do you have any here I could have a look at? It would help with the visuals. Pictures of Salento and the plantation and the Salinas family. And your crew. I have this mental image of Grant as a great bear of a man and would love to know if I'm right.'

Her smile was uncomplicated, her queries straightforward, but the ability to give any answers was anything but. The magazine had taken copies of any of the Colombia photos within his camera, but he hadn't had the chance, or the inclination, to scan or delete them. The images pressed to the back of his mind were vivid enough without stumbling upon photographic evidence.

'No pictures on me I'm afraid. Now tell me, how many pages have we done?' he asked.

She blinked a couple of times at the sudden change of subject before pressing a couple of buttons on her keyboard. 'Around four thousand words computer count, which is a fair effort. And you're right, Salento does sound like an extra-ordinary place. Maybe one day when I get that passport and my own quazillions I can start there.'

She glanced up at him, all heavy-eyed with mussed hair from constantly brushing it away from her face. Half of him wanted to offer to give her a personal guided tour, while the other half wanted to hold her back kicking and screaming from ever setting foot in the place.

But he held it all in. Adding another stratum to the psychological ropes pulling tight around his chest.

'So do I get a cut?' she asked. She twirled her thick hair into a high tight bun before letting it slide and tumble about her shoulders. He wondered what it would feel like against his rough palms. What it would smell like if he buried his face in its length. How close he would have to allow himself to get to her in order to forget everything else.

'A cut of what?' he asked.

She ran her left thumb hard up her right palm again and again. 'The book deal. I've decided I'm getting the raw end of the deal here.'

Hud felt a smile drift up from deep inside of him and pull at his cheek muscles. 'What did you have in mind? Free use of my tennis court? My pool table? Three nights a week in the massive claw-footed bath tub in my bedroom?'

Kendall's eyes grew wide. 'Stuff the percentage. Give me tub time and I'm all yours.'

Her words hung on the air between them as though caught in an invisible web. Big, obvious, complicated, tempting. Her thumb moved to the insides of her fingers pressing them back with more vigour than was likely to be helpful.

Hud did the polite thing and dragged his gaze away from her mortified eyes to her hands. 'You're hurting. Enough for today, I think.'

She stopped massaging her palm and sat on her hands. 'I'm fine.'

'Nah,' he said. 'We have a long way to go yet before this deal is done. So let's put this morning down to a good start, a warm-up of sorts, and you can go have your swim, while I…'

What? Walk in circles? Think too much? Pray that tomorrow I wake up and feel like the old me?

He breathed in deep through his nose. 'While I re-acquaint myself with Claudel's nooks and crannies.'

Kendall pulled herself to her feet. Slowly. Her muscles would be stiff from sitting in the same place for so long. She collected her things as she asked, 'Always the adventurer, aren't you?'

She glanced his way, a potent glimmer in her eye. She had spirit, and a natural inquisitiveness tempered by her comparative inexperience. He wished he could summon even a tenth of that wonder again.

She edged around the desk, then stopped when she was a good metre away from him. She held out her hand, palm up, and presented him with a small rectangular gift.

'A memory stick,' she said. 'I'll back everything up on to it for you every day. For safe keeping.'

'Thanks.' He reached out and slid the small black token from her hand, his finger bumping gently against her soft palm. 'See you tomorrow, same time.'

'Shall do,' she said. Then she turned and left the way she'd come.

Hud moved in the opposite direction, to the front window of the over-sized sitting room, looking out at the white gravel drive and over-grown front garden, holding the still warm memory stick between his palms telling himself over and over why it would be wisest not to follow her.

Even though it meant that the next hour his gut would become a seething knot of sexual tension, knowing she was only fifty metres away, decked out in black Lycra, her hair trailing behind her like wet silk, water caressing her skin exactly as he'd wanted to do since the minute he'd seen her waiting for him at his back door.

Twenty minutes later, Kendall stood at the far end of the pool house.

Patches of sunlight shone through the bougain-villea and dust dappled the water and reflected on to the walls, making the whole area seem as if it was in constant motion. It was a haven of cool and peace and unblemished memory, far away from the fast-moving crazy world and now scorching heat outside.

Once stripped of her boots and clothes and down to her swimsuit, she moved to the edge of the pool, her toes curled around the smooth worn tiles, her skin tightening as she readied herself to dive into the cool water.

Some people inched in. Others dive-bombed to take the edge off the sharp sting of temperature change against their skin. Kendall always liked to dive gracefully, cleanly, with little sound and no splash. For the pool was her one place where she could be elegant. Where she would never be clumsy or off-balanced.

Though this time, as she braced herself, the feeling of anticipation was tinged with…something other. The knowledge that she wasn't alone.

Hud was still inside the house. She had no doubt he would leave her be. He was a gentleman. A gentleman she had caught watching her with something other than gentlemanly thoughts on more than one occasion. A gentleman who could be pushy and fearless. But one who would adhere to her wishes. She'd put what little savings she had on that.

But he knew she was here dressed in nothing bar black Lycra. Knew she would soon be floating, face up, buoyed by the water, her limbs relaxing, her whole body wet and slick, her ears filled with water until she heard nothing but the slap of minute waves on the concrete walls of the pool.

Just as she knew he would be pacing in that grand house of his, all sorts of wars and worries she had no hope of deciphering going on behind those dark hooded eyes.

Alone with their thoughts, they were thinking of one another. She had not one single doubt about it. The doubts plaguing her then and there were of an entirely different nature. Doubts as to her own sanity in allowing such a man to get under her skin.

She took a deep breath and let the light scent of chlorine and palm leaves relax her. For the reason she had fallen for this pool and was willing to do anything not to let it go, had nothing to do with electrolytes, or any desire to win any kind of race. It had everything to do with the tightness, and ache, and fatigue in her heavily scarred, never quite repaired left leg which, after sitting in the same position for so long, had gone beyond discomfort to throbbing pain.

But there was no reason whatsoever for big, handsome Hud Bennington to know any of that. The thought of seeing pity in his eyes in the place of a much more elevating sexual interest made her chest ache as much as her leg.

A man like him could have any woman he

wanted. Perhaps he wanted the woman in his sights at any given moment and if she'd been any other random girl he'd be projecting the same curiosity. Nevertheless, his attention was like a drug and she was fast becoming addicted.

She had to stop this. Stop reading more into his expression than simple inquisitiveness. He was nothing to her. A practical stranger. Someone she had to deal with in order to get what she needed. A traveller here on a short stopover. A ship passing in the night. And far worse for her health than a lack of aqua-therapy.

Without another thought, she lifted on to her toes, closed her eyes and leapt.

CHAPTER FIVE

KENDALL was so far away in a dream world that she flinched when Taffy slammed the front door after coming home from work that night.

Orlando, who'd been sitting on Kendall's left foot at the time, got such a fright at Kendall's sudden movement that he snorted, dragged himself to his feet and left the room.

'Honey,' Taffy called out, 'I'm home!' She left a trail of bags and shoes and jacket on the way from the front door to the desk in the corner in the lounge room where Kendall was sitting. She said, 'So I'm thinking tomorrow I take a sickie and we go into Melbourne. Mama needs a new pair of shoes.'

'Can't,' Kendall said. 'I'm busy tomorrow.' She blinked to clear the fuzz from her eyes and stared back at the Word file on her computer with its several lines highlighted in orange—figures she had to triple-check and log her sources.

'Busy?' Taffy said, slumping into a chair at the dining table. 'And that is code for…?'

Kendall gave up on her work and spun to face Taffy. She hooked her right foot up on to her chair and wrapped her arms around her knee.

'I've made a deal with Hud Bennington,' she said. 'I'm spending my mornings helping him write his memoirs, and for that I get to use the pool whenever I please.' She closed her eyes tightly and waited for a verbal explosion *à la* Taffy. When none came she opened one eye.

'Right.' Taffy nodded as though it all made sense. 'So you and Hud…'

'Have a business arrangement. All business. Super-professional.' Knowing she was protesting far too much, Kendall pushed her wheeled chair over to her best friend and grabbed her hand. 'Why don't you come over tomorrow and I'll re-introduce you like you wanted me to in the first place? And then the two of you can fall in love and get married and I can use the pool whenever I want to anyway.'

'He asked about me?' Taffy said, eyes wide with shock.

'Sure he did. He remembered you as…vivacious.'

Taffy's wide eyes narrowed. 'So he's single.'

'I…think so.'

'But you don't know. You didn't ask. And he

didn't exactly profess undying love for the freckled teenager who used to follow him around like a bad smell.'

'Fine, I have no idea if he's single,' Kendall admitted. Though, if her rusty instincts were anything to go by, he was very much single and had been for some time. Despite whoever the tattoo on his arm referred to.

Taffy turned Kendall's hands over and clasped them. 'It's not every day a girl gets an invite to spend time with some gorgeous rich guy. There's not one single thing in that there scenario to be afraid of.'

Kendall swallowed, panicking that Taffy understood far too clearly why she was begging her to catch Hud's eye. 'That's not what this is, Taffy—'

'Shut up. Seriously. Your eyes are gleaming. Your cheeks have more colour in them than I've ever seen. So if that's not what this is, then I damn well hope that's what this becomes. Unless, of course, in the last ten years Hud's developed a beer belly and a smoker's cough, then I might have to rethink things.' Taffy raised an eyebrow, waiting for confirmation.

There was no getting out of this. The girl was relentless. So Kendall tilted her chin, looked Taffy in the eye and said, 'Fine. You win. He's gorgeous, Taff. He's larger than life. All rugged good looks.

Life lived to the full aura. He's sharp, and wry, and beautiful. Happy now?'

Taffy grinned and pinched Kendall on the cheek. 'That's my girl. So what the hell are you doing here when you could be over there wooing the rich probably single guy?'

'I have no intention of *wooing* him.'

'Why on earth not?' Taffy crossed her arms and glared. 'Did you not say you think him *beautiful*?'

Kendall wished she hadn't been quite so effusive. 'I think Keats' poetry is beautiful. I think Doc Marten boots are beautiful. I think Queen Anne furniture and the pine forest at dawn and bumble-bees are beautiful. Doesn't mean I plan on wooing any of them either.'

'But Hud Bennington is no bumble-bee. I know you far too well, Kendall York. You've thought. You've fantasized. You've pictured yourself in that big beautiful house surrounded by all those beautiful things, wrapped in the arms of that beautiful man. And then you've said, *No, never, not me, after what happened to my last boyfriend, I don't deserve such things,* and dismissed it out of hand.'

Kendall stared at her friend, open-mouthed. 'I have no intention of wooing the guy because he's transient. And insulated. And kind of…damaged, I think. I can feel it lurking behind the smiles and jokes. And he has this tattoo on his shoulder. A woman's name. So, that's that.'

'Rubbish,' Taffy said.

'Rubbish?' Kendall shot back. *'Rubbish?'*

'This has nothing to do with some random tattoo that could be dedicated to his mother for all you know. You aren't letting yourself go for it because of George.' Taffy's statement was direct, but her voice was suddenly soft. So soft Kendall couldn't find it within herself to be outraged. 'It's been three years, Kendall. Crap happened. He didn't survive the accident, but you did. It's time you stopped feeling guilt-ridden and prove it.'

'I—'

'You're a hot chick. You're young. Healthy. In need of a haircut and a stylist, even though that Titian thing you've got going on makes half the guys at my office find you so enchanting it makes me barf. You live in the land of the retiree, so you're in with a shot with any guy who passes this way. It's time to let all that go, Kendall. Beyond time. And from the look of you, that gooey faraway look that shifts over your face when you say his name, this is the guy who could help you do it.'

'But he's leaving as soon as he—'

'I'm not saying marry the guy. Just take this chance to get back on the horse, so to speak.'

'Not that it's any of your business, but since

George I've *been* back on the horse and as a grieving process it wasn't all it was cracked up to be.'

'I don't even mean sex, my sweet young thing. Friendship, attraction, a relationship, love…'

But Kendall just shook her head so hard her brain hurt. Those things made their mark on a person—a mark that couldn't be washed away with a long shower. Hud was the last person she could afford to risk her feelings on. He would leave. And she would hurt. There was no other possible outcome, and it was an outcome she couldn't do again. No high highs meant no low lows and that was that.

'But I don't think I have it in me to go through all the fawning and crushing and coming home and sighing to you every night as you've done to me a thousand times,' she said, changing tack to try to get through to Taffy another way.

Taffy laughed. 'Welcome to the world of the twenty-something single girl. Finally!'

'It's not as much fun as you always said it would be.'

'Of course not. Or nobody would join up. But so long as you have your friends around you to help you over the humps, then you'll be fine.' Taffy sighed. 'It seems my love for Hud Bennington has been thwarted once more. I will now take the hint and move on.'

'But Taffy—'

'No,' Taffy said, peeling herself from the chair and swanning to the arched open doorway with her hand to her forehead. 'I shall have to wallow in the fact that Jonesy at work has finally asked me out on a date.'

'You're kidding!' Kendall said, gripping the arms of her chair. Taffy had been in love with Jonesy, the senior accountant at the firm where she worked, for months.

'Yes. Which is why Mama needs a new pair of shoes. Are you sure you can't come shopping with me?'

Kendall thought about it. Shopping in Melbourne, traipsing through shop after shop, up stairs, across cobbled lanes, until her leg killed. Or stay, and spend another few hours alone with Hud Bennington.

'Well, maybe I could come,' she said.

Taffy only laughed some more. 'And you don't think I saw that coming from a mile away? Stay, my sweet. Go play with your new friend. And tomorrow night I don't want one single detail left out.'

The next morning Kendall was late.

Hud checked his battered old diving watch. Fifteen minutes late. Which wasn't so late in the grand scheme of things, but it was still making him disproportionately antsy.

He moved through the ground floor of the house, weaving in and out of rooms he hadn't yet seen to since he'd come back.

He ended up in the large kitchen with its huge old-fashioned appliances and wooden slab island bench covered in chips and marks made during a hundred house parties. Now the place had a funny smell. Musty. The old scent of dried roses and fresh bread and warm herbs was missing.

Fay. All that had been Fay. She'd made such an impression on this entire house that the memory of her was everywhere. He stood in the large doorway, trying to think of a place, on which he'd left even half such an indelible mark. And he could not think of one.

His apartment in London was only inhabited around ten weeks of the year between gigs; it always smelt to him like a mix of cleaning products and Chinese takeaway. His rucksack and his camera were the closest thing to a home he had—a frayed khaki bag that any sane person would have thrown away years ago and a piece of electrical equipment he had not once taken out of its case since Colombia.

He ran a hand over his eyes. He knew how the house felt. Empty. As if its insides were so much dust. But he wasn't sure that he was the answer to Claudel's woes any more than it was the answer to his.

And for the first time in months he thought of Marcie. They'd dated in London for a few years when he'd first moved there, seeing each other sporadically when he'd been back in town between assignments. She'd told him over and over again that she was happy with their arrangement and he'd believed her. Until the day she'd collapsed into a torrent of tears across the table at a restaurant in Chelsea, begging him to tell her what she had to do to get him to stay with her.

It was at that moment that he'd learned that he was his parents' son after all. A nomad with no fixed address and no ties holding him back. The kind of person who would always put his own desires first. And he'd hurt someone he'd cared about in the process.

He'd taken greater care since then about who he spent his down time with. Making sure to choose the kind of women who truly did understand that he was a wanderer. Not a challenge. The simple truth was he'd been bitten by wanderlust while still in the womb and had not found anything to make him want to stay in one place longer than he had to.

He glanced at his watch. Kendall was eighteen minutes late. He wondered briefly how he had segued so readily from one subject to the other.

The tardy Kendall York was irrelevant to his long term plans, despite the way she invaded his dreams, and his ego with those longing looks she did her very best to hold back. And she was just so lovely that a man could fast lose himself within all that soft skin and never find his way out again.

But he had every intention of finding his way out. Out of this place. Out of this funk. And out there, in the wild blue yonder, where real life really happened.

This place was so far from real life he may as well be living inside one of the Enid Blyton or CS Lewis books he'd read as a kid. All this peace and quiet and tangled beauty was making him feel disconcerted.

At a crossroads he spun on his heel and turned right rather than left down the long hall, took the first staircase he found and ended up in a big square room in which beige velvet curtains with gold tassels covered two of the four walls. He was in the library.

He remembered loving this room when he was a kid. The ceiling-high ladder on wheels had been a big plus for a child with too much energy and a risk addiction. He moved past the mounds of furniture beneath still more dust-covered white sheets until he reached the right-hand wall. He tugged on the long twisted velvet rope and only hoped the whole thing wouldn't fall down upon his head. But the curtains slid aside as though the rail had been oiled that morning, revealing a thousand leather- and paper-bound spines. Some glossy, several threadbare tomes protected behind glass, but all neat, not one out of place.

Kendall would go nuts for this room, he thought. He imagined her, wide-eyed, hand raised, wanting to touch but hesitant, glancing sideways at him, the wonder in her luminous blue-grey eyes making him feel as if he had all her future happiness in the palm of his hand.

He ran his fingers gently over the spines of the books. They were organised, as far as he could tell, with no regular rhyme or reason. Knowing Fay, it could have been the order in which she'd bought them, or read them, or loved them. Many names were familiar and some not so much— Chaucer, Francis, Christopher, Neels, Bradbury…

And one William Shakespeare.

Hud stopped, his eyes roving over the curly gold script of several volumes until he found what he was looking for.

He slid the leather bound copy of *Henry V* from its slot, then roamed to the middle of the room and absently slid the white sheet away from a long red velvet chaise longue and let it flutter to the floor, the wafting dust now feeling somehow normal.

He sat, found the proposal scene between King Henry and Katherine and read. And read. And read, as the King, knowing himself to be naught but a plain soldier at heart, set about wooing the beautiful, stubborn and purposely ambiguous princess by asking she *clap hands and a bargain* and agree to become his wife.

He leant back against the hard old chair, crossed his foot atop his knee and felt the humour of the scene slide through him. Kendall was right—he did laugh. He didn't cry, thank goodness. And his heart didn't exactly go pitter-pat. But something in the dust-enriched vacuum around that particular organ connected with the King who knew he was unable to recommend himself to anyone as anything other than the exact man he was.

Hud let the book drop to his lap and stared blindly across the room. *Take me…take a Soldier, take a King.* If you want me, take me as I am.

He ran a hand across his jaw. Would the day ever come when he used that same sentiment to explain himself to a woman? When he looked for the comfort of having a witness to his life? One person who knew all of his stories. Someone to lean on when the time came to leave a party early. Someone to give him a reason to come home from the front.

He shot from his chair and strode over to the wall to slide the book back firmly into place.

Family? A wife? Dinner parties? Who was he kidding? The world was his home. And he was only here, now, to convince his bosses that he was ready to go back out there. To flea-ridden beds. Rock-covered ground. Tents in places where it rained more in a day than it rained in a whole year in Melbourne.

Yeah. His path was chosen. The sooner Kendall was here to help him get his story out of his head the better. So why then had she, of all people, the one woman who continuously knocked him further and further off course by simply existing, been put smack bang in the middle of that path? Maybe, before he could do anything else, he would have to find that out for sure.

He looked at his watch again and tilted his head to see if he could hear her in the house. But it was as quiet as a country church.

Needing her, and soon, he made to leave, to go looking for her. But on the way, as though pressed by some voice in the back of his head telling him to get over himself and allow the house to take a real deep breath, he grabbed every sheet off every piece of furniture in the library, bundling them up into a great ball and took them out of the room with him as he left.

Kendall rushed up to Hud's back door, her breathing hot and fast as she had run through the forest to get there as fast as she could. She stretched out her left leg so that it wouldn't completely lock up when her muscles cooled.

When she reached up to knock on the back door she found it ajar. Reminding her she was almost an hour later than she had been the day before.

She bustled inside, heading straight for the sitting room, where she found Hud standing at the front window. Her Doc Martens squeaked on the floor as she skidded to a halt. She tried to think of an excuse, a reason that wouldn't seem lame or ridiculous. Perhaps she had errands. Or a sudden deadline. Or Orlando had eaten her laptop.

The truth was she had slept in. After lying in bed staring at the array of glowing plastic stars that covered her ceiling, or standing with her head in the fridge looking for answers to why she couldn't stop replaying every second of the day she had spent with Hud—every delicious reaction to his voice, his looks, his words, his scent, his stories, his amazing life—she'd finally fallen asleep just before dawn. Only after having convinced herself that Hud Bennington was a regular guy—flawed, fleeting and emotionally obstructed. Nothing worth filling pages of her notebook about.

'I'm sooooo sorry I'm late, Hud,' she said, letting her bags slide to the floor by the table.

He turned, pinning her with his dark hazel gaze.

From across the room she saw several emotions flicker across his eyes—relief, foreboding and, finally, blatant attraction.

And every last sensation she'd spent the night hours qualifying came spinning back to her. Every other excuse not to want him may have been dead on, but the man, and the way she felt about him, were anything but regular. What kind of mess had she gone and got herself into?

'It's fine,' he said. 'It's not like I had anywhere else to be. You are the only pressing item on my calendar right now, Kendall.'

The book, she thought frantically. *He means the book is the only thing on his calendar.*

'Still…sorry.' She offered him a smile short on emotion and long on professionalism. At least she hoped that was what she'd done. The guy made her feel so back to front and inside out she could well have grimaced at him and simply not known.

She hurriedly set up her laptop, her pencils and red notebook and sat at the ready. She was glad he was far enough away that he wouldn't see that her hands and knees were shaking.

While waiting for the Word file to load, Kendall pulled her hair away from her neck, twirling it high atop her head to let some cool air wash across her neck, which had begun to scorch the moment Hud had looked her way.

'Right. So where were we up to?' she asked, re-reading the last page from the day before. 'Mostly stuff about the Salinas family.'

Actually so far there had been a heck of a lot about other people and not so much about the author. Which, for a memoir, seemed a little odd. The day before, it had felt as though he was building to something. The growing tension in his shoulders, the need to pace and go off on long tangents while staring long and hard at a hunk of wallpaper for ten minutes straight. Maybe today he'd get to the exciting stuff. The adventures she was longing to hear about. The reasons behind the battered clothes and scar on his lip.

'Are you hot?' Hud asked as he slid into the sofa in her line of vision.

She glanced up. His gaze was roving over her uplifted arms, down the tumble of curls and then back to her face, a slight smile adding creases to the corners of his already unfairly gorgeous eyes. She knew what such a smile meant. It was enough for her to drop her hair in a flash.

'Nope,' she said, back to staring at the monitor and shuffling the mouse for no particular reason. 'If you are, get yourself a cold drink. I can wait.'

She saw him shake his head out of the corner of her eye. 'I'm fine. But I don't dress in heavy boots and long skirts day in and day out.'

'You're giving me fashion advice? I though we'd established yesterday you had no such right.' Kendall gave his T-shirt and jeans and bare feet a haughty once over. Then kind of wished she hadn't. In old jeans and a soft grey polo shirt the guy looked good. Better than good. He looked relaxed. Easygoing. And hot in a whole other meaning of the word.

His shadow of a smile kicked up a notch as though her every thought was written across her face. 'I just want you to be comfortable.' *Around me*, he didn't need to say. But she felt the words clearly.

Hud Bennington may be flawed, fleeting and emotionally obstructed, but he was in no way backward about coming forward. It was as though, during the same time in which she'd made herself promise to pull her tumbling feelings for him back under tighter control, he'd decided the exact opposite.

Well, that would only make her job of ignoring what was happening between them all the more vital.

'I'm beyond comfortable,' she said, eye-balling him. 'So comfortable I've been contemplating dragging that fancy coffee table over here so I can put my feet up.'

Hud's smile only grew and her resistance took a beating. 'If the fancy takes you, go right ahead.'

Kendall glanced down at the no doubt ridiculously pricey antique piece in front of Hud's legs. Intricate patterns were carved into the edges. Curling legs, with French Provincial overtones. She'd never land her clunky boots atop such a piece. It would be sacrilege.

Hud suddenly lifted his right foot from atop his left knee and made to do just that and Kendall sucked in a shaft of air and jerked towards him. His foot hovered. He waited until her wayward eyes locked once more with his.

And then he laughed. Real, natural, out loud laughter that hit the walls and came back again. He held a hand to his stomach as though it was painful and unexpected. She felt his relief and release in the laughter as strongly as if it were her own. Her empathy towards him was so potent it left an aftertaste like one of Taffy's infamous Amaretto biscuits. Bitter, sweet and lasting.

'You can be very trying, Mr Bennington,' Kendall said.

'And you, Ms York, are not nearly as impervious and tough as you'd like me to think you are.'

'I'm plenty tough,' she shot back. And to prove it she turned back to the computer and rested her fingers lightly on the keyboard, ignoring all that visual inducement a meagre two metres in front of her. 'Just you try to put your dirty foot on that gorgeous table and you'll see just how tough.

Now, if you want to get any story-telling done today, you'd better get cracking. I have a date with a pool that I have no intention of missing.'

'Right,' he said. 'We could do that.'

Kendall's shoulders slumped as she let go of a melodramatic sigh. The guy really wasn't making this any easier for her.

'Or?' she asked.

'It's too hot to sit in here. And far too nice outside to let such a day pass us by.'

'I've seen a hundred such days, Hud. Believe me, we'll both survive missing this.'

Hud dragged his lanky form from the chair and rubbed his hands together. 'Maybe you will, but I've been cooped up in here for days now. I'm going stir crazy. I need to get out of here.'

'And go where, precisely?'

'I don't know. Just out. I'm sure there are places you've never seen. A local boy like me could show you some stuff.'

Kendall raised one eyebrow and feigned utter indifference. 'I've lived here for over three years. I don't know what you could possibly show me that I haven't already seen.'

'You're twenty-three,' he shot back with a winning smile that did nasty things to Kendall's stomach. 'I'm thirty…something. There's plenty a man of my experience could show you.'

'What on earth did you eat for breakfast, Hud?' she asked as he sauntered over to her desk. Her chair made a scraping sound against the floor as she pushed it back in haste to put more space between them. 'Mushrooms, by any chance? Picked from the garden? Or perhaps leaves from a tomato plant that wasn't really a tomato plant at all?'

'Eggs,' he said. 'Bacon. Steaming-hot tomatoes, no leaves attached, delivered by a nice lady called Mrs Jackson from town. It's amazing what you can get at the end of the phone nowadays.'

'Maybe Mrs Jackson would like you to show her around Saffron instead,' Kendall said.

'Nah,' Hud said, holding out a hand to her. 'You'll do just fine.'

He was backlit. So dark, so tall, so different, so engaging, so dangerous. She felt as if he were a knight on a white steed and she a fallen princess. And, just like some girl from a fairy tale, the moment she put her hand in his, her life would never be the same again.

She baulked—not in the least bit ready for that kind of pressure. She didn't want her life to change. It had taken years to finally feel content. Or as content as she could hope to be.

'This book of yours won't write itself, Hud.'

'More's the pity.'

'You're a procrastinator, you know that?'

'Never have been before,' he said. 'I'm usually Mr Gung-Ho. Don't quite know what's happened to change all that.'

She ignored his hand, though she did lift herself out of the chair. She turned off her laptop and closed it. Then stood so that the desk and chair still lay between them.

He moved around the desk, his warm, masculine scent reaching out to her as he came closer. She crossed her arms and did her best to keep the two of them separate islands in the same ocean of hard wood floor.

But the determined look in his eye spoke of as much temptation and danger to her equilibrium, to her hard won contentment, as the offered hand had done. And Kendall wasn't all that sure how much longer she could possibly resist.

'Come on, sunshine,' he said with a laugh, before grabbing her hand anyway and dragging her away.

CHAPTER SIX

HUD tugged Kendall through the old-fashioned family kitchen. Taffy would have had a ball in that room. There must have been three ovens. Kendall's mouth watered at the thought of how many Amaretto biscuits that could bake in one hit.

He grabbed a small cooler bag from the island bench. It had obviously been prepared earlier, before she'd arrived. So this excursion was not nearly so sudden a thought as he'd been making out.

Kendall held tight to Hud's hand as he dragged her out into the blinding sunshine and around the side of the house. Or perhaps he was holding tight to her. Either way, somehow her hand had stayed in his. And it fitted. Perfectly. All safely tucked inside his large strong mitt.

'Is it too soon to ask again where you are taking me?'

'Trust me, you'll love it,' Hud said, before pulling her hand across his torso so that her hip knocked against his side and her arm slid across his stomach. The feel of bunched muscles and his inner heat made the hairs on her arms stand on end.

When they reached a garden shed, Hud let her go. She wrapped her left hand in her right, holding the warmth therein as long as she could.

He pulled open the creaking metal door. She sneezed about eight times at the amount of dust that puffed out into the sunshine, which saw its first chance for escape in a decade and wasn't wasting any time.

She followed him just inside the door to find the shed was huge, with a high canted roof, and dents and holes and cracks enough for slivers of sunlight to pour faint light upon stacks of old boxes, half a dozen fishing rods, croquet mallets and balls. And Hud, picking his way over piles of who knew what to get to something that had caught his eye at the very back.

Kendall stayed in the doorway and watched as an impressive expanse of tanned skin peeked out from below Hud's faded polo shirt. *It's only skin*, she told herself as a wave of pure feminine pleasure fanned out from the centre of her stomach.

He spun then, holding his prize upside down and aloft in a pair of arms with muscles clenching and bulging magnificently under the weight of it.

The hint of the tattoo of another woman's name peeking out from beneath the sleeve of his shirt.

'It's a bike,' she said, the obvious about all she could muster in that moment.

'It's a bike,' he agreed, grinning from ear to ear. 'And…'

'And you and I are going for a ride,' he said, picking his way back through the junk.

'You told me to trust you. You promised I would love your surprise. Uh-uh. No, thanks. Not my scene.' She backed out of the shed so fast she almost tripped over an upturned wrought iron garden bench.

Hud's face dropped, and so did the bike, until he was watching her over the top of the dusty tyres and wheel spokes, looking like a puppy who'd just been told he was a naughty boy.

'I…' How could she put this and not make a complete fool of herself? Her left leg… She simply couldn't… 'I can't ride, Hud. I never learned.'

'Oh,' he said. 'Well, that's okay. You don't have to. I've ridden this thing more times with a girl on the handlebars than not, so we'll be fine.'

Right. Of course he had. Taffy had been in love with him at the age of thirteen. It was likely that every other local female with two eyes in her head had as well.

'That's supposed to make me feel better? That

I'll be the one hundred and first *girl* you've let ride on your handlebars?'

Hud watched her for a few seconds. In silence. Loaded silence. The back of Kendall's neck began to prickle when he stepped over the last of the obstacles, bike in hand, and ambled her way.

'That's not exactly what I was trying to say,' he said. 'We have sun. We have fresh air. We have picnic food. We have ways and means of using the bike to make the most of the small pleasures afforded to us on this day. I was not trying to give you the chance to summon up some girly reason to say no.'

By that stage Hud was so close that Kendall could see the flecks of gold in his eyes. So close she could smell his woodsy scent over the top of the dust and mould in the crowded space. So close she could hear the nuanced notes in his voice. Reason. Laughter. Flirtation.

'Girly?' Kendall repeated, surprised to find her voice had suddenly grown husky. 'Being that I am twenty-three does not make me a babe in arms. It means that I am a grown woman, and it has been some years since I have done anything close to *girly*.'

Hud smiled, his eyes roving over her long loose hair, her pale green and beige layered tank-tops and favoured flared ankle-length skirt, this one chocolate, and her nicest if she was prepared to admit it, before lifting again to focus on her cheeks, which she knew were growing pinker by the second. 'Just calling it like I see it.'

The old bike lay easily in his strong arms, hovering between them like a shield. Tension crackled through the dust soaked air. Sexual tension. Pure and unadulterated. So thick Kendall felt it sparking in her lungs with every inward breath. Humming through her chest. Warming her belly.

Drunk on the sensation, she stuck out a hip and her right hand landed square upon it, fingers splayed. He had no idea, but *that* was the most purposefully *girly* move she had made in a heck of a long time. 'You obviously missed my point. I was pointing out how clueless you are.'

'All I heard was the distinct purr of jealousy.'

'Of the kinds of girls who'd ride a guy's handlebars? Hardly.'

'Don't knock it until you try it.'

'Did Mirabella ever try it?' The second the words left her mouth Kendall wished she could take them back. She was swimming in deeper waters than she was used to and now felt as if she'd swallowed a mouthful of salt water.

'Who?' Hud asked, his gaze far sharper than his words.

'Don't play dumb. I saw your tattoo yester-day.' She flicked a hand in the general direction of his right arm.

His face split into a huge grin and she wished she hadn't asked. If Mirabella turned out to be some glorious Amazonian goddess he was madly in love with she might just cry. Even though she knew that ought to make her feel far better than if Mirabella turned out to be his mother, and he was in fact totally single…

'Mirabella is my camera,' he said. 'Same one I've had for five years now. And as much a part of my success as any kind of talent I might have. Hence the tattoo.'

Kendall tried to come up with a comeback or a clever remark which would make her look less like a woman who'd just admitted she was jealous of a piece of electronic equipment, but the only words knocking about in her suddenly wide open mind were, 'Then fine. I'll do it. I'll ride your stupid handlebars.'

Hud's eyebrows shot north. 'Well, that was easier than I expected.'

'Don't get used it,' she said.

'I really could, you know.'

'I'll bet.' She moved out of his way so that he and his bike could get past. And so that she could take a breath without drinking in his essence at the same time. 'So where are you taking me on this trip back down memory lane?'

'Let that be a surprise too.'

'Shall I wear my poodle skirt and pigtails like the girls of your long *long* ago youth? Or did you go for the bad girls? Skinny black jeans and torn T-shirts? Should I get a pack of cigarettes to shove up my sleeve?'

'Not so much hard work involved, in fact. I always went for the smart girls. So you may as well come as you are.'

His precisely aimed point hit deep, lodging somewhere behind her left breast. She tied imaginary ropes around her ribs to keep her heart from thumping so hard in her chest it left a mark. And she summoned up a hearty glare as she said, 'Another example of your subtlety. And that you are as clueless as you were five minutes ago.'

'Well, prepare yourself, my sweet. Only practise makes perfect.' He hitched the bike on to his shoulder like some kind of he-man and grinned at her some more.

It was just so ridiculous, the house-bound adventurer and the town-bound girl who had learned the hard way that adventure was best left for other people, squaring off over a twenty-year-old bicycle. But she was here now, the sun was shining and the thought of doing something so daring as riding a boy's handlebars was too tempting to pass up.

The growing pleasure at the idea could be her little secret. It didn't mean she was reverting back to the freewheeler she'd been once upon a time. It was just one time, one day.

'Now come on, Butch Cassidy,' she said. 'Let's get going on that bike of yours before I change my mind.'

Warm summer air slid through Kendall's hair and her eyes watered as Hud pedalled away from the main road and down the bumpy dirt path that took them to Saffron Falls after which the township had been named.

Her hands gripped the handlebars on the outside of her backside, which was beginning to go numb from sitting on such a tiny piece of metal for a good twenty minutes. Her teeth clenched and rattled with every bump. But she closed her eyes and let the scent of moss and grass and dust settle over her. The sun beat down on her shoulders and the backs of her eyelids. The whistle of the wind filled her ears until she felt as if she were flying.

Weightless. Just like when she went swimming. But better. Fully clothed. Out and about in the big wide world. Wild. Free. Full of possibility. She didn't want it to end.

The bike slowed and twisted left. Kendall's eyes fluttered open to find they were now under the shade of a dozen willow trees. She ducked so as not to be hit by the fall of soft leaves.

'Nearly there,' Hud said. His voice so clear and so close she could feel it tickling against the back of her neck.

'Thank God,' she said, pulling herself together. 'Five more minutes and I might never regain feeling in my backside.'

The bike slowed a mite further. Kendall dug her boot-clad toes into the mud-guard to keep her balance as they slowed to a halt just as the bike split two curtains of willow leaves to land in a verdant glade. Lush green grass covered lightly undulating ground all the way down to a rocky stream bordered by tall skinny grey gum-trees and willows dipping into a crystal-clear pool of water. The sound of a nearby waterfall whispered on the air.

Hud's foot hit the ground and he reached out an arm around her waist to stop her from falling. Her right hand instinctively wrapped around his arm, holding him tight.

For a few moments she leaned back against him. Her breathing slowed to match his. The light sheen of sweat covering his skin warmed her back. The scent of hot male curled itself around her and seeped deep beneath her ever-weakening defences.

'Well, this is good news,' he said, his voice a low murmur against her left ear. 'It's been so long since I've been here I was beginning to think I was leading us into the wilderness, never to be found again. How are you at hunting and gathering?'

'Never tried. Though since I mastered handlebar riding so quickly I'd imagine I would be brilliant at that too.'

Hud's soft laughter rumbled through her chest as if it were her own.

She felt his other foot thud against the ground. He kept a light hold of her around the waist as he helped her slide away from him and off the front of the bike. The back of her tank-top caught on the front of his T-shirt so that the cotton slid smoothly along her skin.

When her feet hit solid ground, she didn't let go quite quickly enough. He asked, 'You all right?'

She let him go, tugged her clothing back into shape and nodded, not all that sure what her voice might sound like.

She left him to prop the bike against a tree and take the cooler pack off his back while she headed down to the stream. She squatted and ran her fingers through the water to find it was surprisingly cool.

'Hungry yet?' Hud asked.

'Famished.'

'Of course you are. All that hard work hanging on while I merely pedalled.'

'Are you fishing for me to goo and gah at how big and strong you are for lugging my heavy lump of a form around with you?' she asked.

'Are you fishing for me to tell you that you are as light as a feather?'

She stood and glanced over her shoulder. 'Are you saying I'm not?'

'Hell, yeah,' he said. 'You're bloody heavy.'

She spun all the way to face him. 'Of course it could be that you are far older and weaker than you were the last time you did this. I'm not thirteen years old, remember.'

Hud seemed to think about it for a few seconds before saying, 'Nah. That can't be it.'

'Right. You're a big strong man and I'm a lump.'

'I'm happy with that.'

'Hmm.' Kendall moved further away again, along the edge of the stream, taking in her surroundings, but really just needing a break from the thick and fast flirtation they had suddenly found themselves embroiled in. So far she was handling herself okay, but she feared if Hud decided to turn it up a notch she'd trip over her awkwardness.

She moved past the edge of the half-moon-shaped thicket and came face to face with a craggy cliff, covered in ferns and moss and spilt down the centre by a small but picturesque waterfall. It was so charming. Magical, even. She breathed in deeply and silently thanked Hud, and her conscience too, for giving her this day.

'Nice surprise?'

She'd expected Hud to stay back and lay out the picnic, but naturally he was just behind her as she slipped into a vulnerable moment. 'Hud, this is just…' But she couldn't even find the words.

'Isn't it, though?' He crouched down beside her and ran his fingers through the water where tiny worn round stones disappeared into the deep darkness of a small but perfect lake.

Kendall crossed her arms and stood at the edge of the water, not quite sure how she had ended up here—poised on the edge of a dreamy landscape with gorgeous Hud Bennington at her side.

He stood, his large form seeming to fill the wide space as he tucked his hands in the back pockets of his jeans and looked at her. Just looked at her. While he was surrounded with all the beauty in the world. If she was ever to indulge in any kind of romantic urge, this would be the time.

'Did you used to bring girls here often?' she asked and turned away quickly, mortified at showing just how rusty she was at all this, whatever this was.

But he didn't seem to notice. Taking her

question at face value, he said, 'Some of the local kids and I used to come down here to swim when I summered here. We all thought that nobody else in the world knew about it. Now here I am, all grown up, one of the adults we'd all come here to get away from. And I would hazard a guess that the next generation thinks they are the only ones in the world who know about it now.'

'It's the way the world turns,' Kendall said.

'It is. Faster and faster as the years go by. So fast I find myself feeling like I have to run faster and faster to simply keep up.'

Kendall felt her breath tighten in her lungs. For that was an actual honest-to-goodness revelation from the man she'd convinced herself was an emotional clam shell. 'I used to feel like that.'

He turned to her and lifted one eyebrow. 'You did?'

She knew he was asking because she was twenty-three and he was thirty…something. As if God kindly put a moratorium on bad things happening to a person until one was at least a quarter of a century old. The guy might be worldly, but his blinkers were as big as anyone else she'd ever met.

'Big time,' she admitted. 'I ran so fast and so hard for a while the edges of my life became a complete blur. Losing your place, your purpose, your footing. Ever happened to you?'

Hud merely blinked, slowly, and if anything he was suddenly paying her more attention. His dark hazel eyes looking deeper into hers, weighing her every word with care.

She looked back out at the peaceful waterfall. 'I simply made the decision to plant my feet on solid ground and running became redundant.'

She was about to say, *You should try it*, but the words lodged in her throat. They were talking in sweeping statements right now. Specifics would be too much like admitting she'd thought long and hard about what might happen between them if by some miracle he stayed.

'Want to tell me what sent you running in the first place?' he asked, his deep sexy voice making her want to tell him everything—about her wild teenage years without parental influence of any kind, about George's calming influence and how her nature had won out and she'd gone and ruined everything—more than she'd ever wanted to before. But she couldn't bear to see the look in his eyes. That mixture of sympathy and judgement.

'Want to tell me what really happened to you in Colombia?' she threw back, wondering just how far he was prepared to share.

He laughed softly. 'Mmm, I did say I always went for the smart ones, did I not? You'd think a guy would learn.' He was ducking and swerving.

She should know. She'd could have gone pro in the sport years ago.

He said, 'How about we head back and picnic before my stomach rumbles overtake the gorgeous sound of that waterfall?'

Or before either of us step over the obvious but thinning line keeping us at a safe distance from one another? Kendall thought.

As they made their way back to the thicket, she wondered which one of them would trip first.

After lunch of cold chicken and a basic salad which Hud had rustled up from the magical delivering Mrs Jackson from town, Kendall splayed herself out on the grass—spreadeagled, full and gorgeously lethargic. As if giving herself permission to relax, her body had taken her at her word and become a mass of rubber.

'Did you ever have a nickname at school?' Hud asked.

Kendall turned her head to find him lying on his side, his chin on his hand, stretched out across a patch of soft springy grass like a satiated Labrador. 'I'm not telling you that.'

'And why not?

'Because you'll use it against me.'

'Mine was a charming take on the "third" part of my name.'

Kendall could only imagine. 'Fine. Mine was Ken Doll.'

'Mmm,' Hud said, turning to hold himself up by his elbows as he looked out over the stream. 'Kids can be so inventive.'

'Yours was far worse.'

'Nah, I made that up just so you'd spill.'

Kendall laughed and her full stomach groaned. 'You're a piece of work.'

'That I am. Want to go for a swim?' he asked, adding Groucho Marx eyebrows for good measure.

'Ah, no.'

'Why not? I've never met anyone as in love with the pastime as you. Surely the electrolytes in a pond would be far better for you than any in a pool.'

'Actually, I made that up too.'

'Noooo,' he said, eyes comically wide. 'I don't believe it.'

'Mmm-hmm. I was embarrassed to say that I use your pool to help keep my skin silky-soft and looking years younger than I *really* am.'

'So you're not really twenty-three, then. That's an interesting turn.'

'Yep,' she said. 'The truth is, I'm old enough that you could be my son.'

Hud let his head fall back as he laughed, that full-throated, big man laugh of his that made her feel fragile and girly and made her stomach flip and tumble. Every time. 'God, that's depressing.'

'Thought it might be.'

'So,' he said, a smile still firmly in place, 'how about that swim? Stay in your underwear if you like. I promise I won't look.'

Something in the way he said it made Kendall imagine that if she took to the woods to strip he'd know exactly which way to turn to find a nice reflective surface if he so desired. She felt her very toes begin to blush.

She instinctively tugged her skirt lower at the thought of getting semi-naked in Hud's presence again, but that had nothing to do with her toes whatsoever. And everything to do with what else lay beneath the long discreet folds of thick cotton.

She'd forgotten. For one beautiful hour in Hud's presence, she'd completely forgotten. She'd allowed herself to simply revel in the precarious feeling of being the kind of girl a man like Hud Bennington 'went for'.

But, no matter what, no matter how far she allowed herself to indulge in the feelings he aroused in her, in the knowledge that she was getting closer and closer to the real man behind the mask, the man she had glimpsed that first day in the pool house, the soulful man, when it came down to it she had far more to hide.

He had a scar above his lip. It made him seem even sexier and slightly dangerous, which would have sent any sensible girl running for the hills. Problem was, she was beginning to realise that, despite her safe house, her ordered life, her nice job, she was not the sensible girl she so tried to be. While she…while her left leg…there was nothing remotely sexy about it.

'I have no interest in heading back home in wet underwear,' she said, her voice far cooler than she felt. 'And, before you even suggest it, I have less interest in swimming yet not getting my underwear wet in the first place.'

'Your loss,' he said.

She heard movement from his patch of grass. She squinted in case he suddenly decided to whip his T-shirt over his head, pop the fly of his jeans, unzip so loud it would echo off the cliff walls and de-trouser. She imagined it in great detail. His hard pecs golden from a thousand suns, a sprinkling of dark hair covering his chest and threading to an arrow point at the top edge of his pants and a pair of long, sculpted, muscular, masculine legs.

She pulled herself into a sitting position, then opened one eye and risked a sideways glance to find him fully dressed and watching her with a small smile on his face. She cleared her throat and very purposefully looked out across the beautiful vista.

'Hud, why did you really bring me here?' She'd actually meant to ask why they weren't back at his place writing this book he was apparently so desperate to get finished. But instead she'd accidentally asked the question she'd really wanted to. 'I mean, I—'

'Can't you just relax and enjoy the moment?' Hud eased himself down on to the grass with an excessive groan, leaving one bent knee pointed skyward.

Kendall's heart rate doubled at the sight of clenching forearms and thigh muscles straining against denim. 'Apparently not,' she muttered.

'If you must know, I remembered this place this morning,' he said. 'One of a thousand old memories I haven't thought of in years that have been swimming back to me over the past few days, and I just wanted to come out here and see if it was as spectacular as I remembered.'

She tucked her right leg beneath her while keeping her left relatively straight. 'You should have brought your camera. Mirabella,' she added for good measure.

A smile creased his cheeks. 'Perhaps I should have.'

'I would have thought that having your camera

on you would be as hard to forget as my having a pen and notepaper.'

'Did you bring your notebook?'

'I would have if you'd given me the chance to get my bag. I actually feel kind of naked without it.'

Hud left that thought to bounce on the breeze awhile so that both of them contemplated the word *naked* far longer than necessary.

But then his next words explained his long silence far better. 'I work with people who are more into recording life than living it. Like tourists who burn through Europe with a video camera strapped to their right eye socket. I can't quite reconcile that thought process with what I know of you.'

Kendall laughed softly. 'What you *think* you know of me after four days.'

'Look who's counting,' Hud said, equally softly. He was back lying on his side by this stage, holding up his head with his right hand.

He was right. She knew him as little as he knew her, yet she felt as if she'd known him for ever. As if they'd met again and again over a hundred life-times, circling, and seeking, and wondering, and never quite managing to step through the looking-glass into one another's world. Would this be another of those times? Or would one of them be strong enough to take the leap into the unknown?

He was right. And he was intriguing. And so very tormentingly beautiful, she thought. Like an apparition. Like something she had dreamed up in her lonely moments lying in bed at night, wishing her life had turned out differently.

But differently surely should have meant that she married George. Sweet, amenable, funny George. Whose eye colour she couldn't quite remember, even if she closed her eyes tight against the darkness and thought back with all her might. George, whose voice she used to recognise one word into a phone conversation, though now she wondered if it had ever really been that way or her mind was playing tricks.

'It's not about recording rather than living,' she finally said. 'You just forget. Even the important things eventually fade. No matter how hard you try to hang on, the tiny details turn to dust, and the significant moments become nothing more animated than a photograph. So now I write those details down. Just in case. Because some things it's your duty to remember.'

'Such as?' Hud asked.

She hesitated. Then convinced herself this wasn't stepping over the line into familiarity; it was just conversation. 'I started my first notebook when I was eight. That's when my mother died. I began to find that I was forgetting things about her already. I began to write down silly memories. It helped. And it stuck.'

He watched her for a few long moments before saying, 'My parents were anthropologists. They studied forgotten civilisations. They would have loved it if there were more people like you keeping track of everyday life.'

'Did they travel a lot too?' she asked, finding herself trying to piece Hud together despite herself.

'Constantly,' he said. 'I travelled with them until school age. Then I went to boarding school and stayed with Aunt Fay every summer. They planned to take me with them for my gap year after graduation but they died on location, a rock slide in Guatemala, my last year of high school.'

'Hmm. My father wasn't there for me all that much after Mum died. He was around, but just not there in any real sense. He tried, but it can't have been easy.'

The two of them let their intimate confessions ease into one another's consciousness. Like pieces of a puzzle sliding neatly into place, Kendall saw how Hud had followed in his parents' footsteps. Had she done the same as her father? Dimming the light of her life to deal with the loss of love? Were these responses in the blood? Inevitable? Inescapable?

'Are you guys close now?' Hud asked before she could come to any sort of set conclusion.

'Not so much. Christmas phone calls and birthday cards. He has remarried. Has a new family now.' She shook her head and took a deep breath. 'How can this stuff still matter so much when we are grown-ups ourselves?'

'Does it really matter?' he asked.

She glanced at him and gave him time enough to figure it out for himself.

'Hell, yeah, it matters,' Hud admitted and they both laughed.

Kendall leant back on her skinny arms, legs tucked away out of the glorious sunshine, looking out into the dark water, her fine profile backlit, showing off the slightest bump in her nose, the luscious natural pout of her lips and a determined furrow in her brow.

Hud shifted his elbow, which had somehow found the only rock on the whole embankment to lean upon. The movement caught her eye. She turned her head his way and blinked.

He smiled, a lazy, easy, just for her smile, and halfway caught between wherever she had mentally been and being fully with him, she let down her guard and smiled right on back.

If he'd ever felt as if he were living through a series of moments that would slip from his memory like quicksilver, these were them. The shift and change of her expressions. The dip of her left eyebrow when she frowned. The crease in her left cheek when she smiled. And the subtle yet important change of colour in her eyes when he said something that made her laugh. There was no way one simple man could keep all of that in his head and leave room to remember to eat, drink and breathe.

She was unique. She was somebody he didn't want to forget as he seemed to have forgotten so much else in his non-stop life. Perhaps he needed to do something memorable so that when he left she would not be able to forget him either.

If he reached out with his free hand he would be able to touch her foot—well, her shoe at least. And perhaps slide his hand north to enclose his fingers around her slim ankle. Skin on skin. He'd know then, by the revealing darkening of her eyes, if she was ready for him to go further.

'Is that how you see your photos?' she asked as though a good three minutes of silence hadn't passed since their last words. And the moment, the chance to touch her, dissolved away. 'Ways to capture moments that will never happen again?'

She looked at him, all apple cheeks and soft pink lips and bedroom eyes. If only he had Mirabella with him now... If only the very thought of lifting the black metallic weight in his hands again didn't give him the shakes.

He cleared his throat. 'Not quite so romantic as all that, I'm afraid. I get paid to push people's emotional buttons. Though I think I might use your take on my résumé instead.'

'Are you thinking of changing jobs?'

He paused. A nanosecond at most. But he felt it. The indecision, where in the past there had been nothing but rabid compulsion. The tingling impression that lying back in the sunshine, with this woman at his side, baiting him, pushing *his* buttons, was a hell of a lot nicer way to spend his time than lying in three-inch deep cold water in a Vietnamese rice paddy.

'Are you?' she asked.

'Nah. It's all I know how to do.' He dragged himself upright, stood and brushed grass from his jeans, trying to brush away the hazy, lazy feelings usurping his need to keep on the move. 'Now, if we're not going swimming, and there's no more food, I'm thinking it might be time for us to head back.'

He reached out a hand to her, to help her up. He once again saw the war in her eyes as she decided whether or not that would be a smart move. She shifted, wincing as though her leg had gone numb beneath her. He knew it was another ruse so as not to touch him.

He grinned. 'Come on, Kendall. Take my hand. I promise I'll give it back.'

With a grimace more pained than was nice to his ego, she did as she was asked. And he only let go of her when he absolutely had to, in order to mount the bike that would take them both back home.

CHAPTER SEVEN

THE ride back to Claudel felt far quicker to Kendall than the ride to Saffron Falls had been. Everything felt as if it were moving faster now. The hours in the day. The usually solid world beneath her feet.

She dismounted more rapidly when they arrived too. All the better to avoid the way his arm had wrapped around her waist the first time, the way their clothes had caught on one another and tugged against her skin, the way her body had slid down his.

She walked away from the bike, the shed, him.

'Hey, are you okay?' Hud called out.

She glanced over her shoulder to find that he had dumped the bike against the shed wall.

'You're limping. I saw you wince back on the grass and I just assumed your leg had fallen asleep.'

With every word he came closer, hands outstretched, face etched with concern. And pity. And oodles of honest-to-goodness caring.

Kendall backed away until one more step would have landed her in a shrub against the side of the house.

'I'm so sorry; was I too rough on the bike?' He reached out and his hand hovered near her waist.

'Nope,' she said, shaking her head, flapping her hands and avoiding eye contact like a pro. 'It's fine. I'm fine. You were right. Nothing bar a dead leg. I just need to walk it off.'

'Come back inside for a bit and sit. I'll get us both a cold drink.'

She did a sidestep until she was no longer blocked in between a rock and hard place, taking great care to lift both feet evenly, her heavy boots helping on that score as usual. 'Better I go now. Busy busy. Life beyond the pine forest to take care of.'

He watched her blather like an idiot. 'Don't you want to get your laptop bag?'

'Why bother? I'll just have to bring it back next time.'

'You don't need your laptop? For life beyond the pine forest?'

Damn. 'Yeah. Yeah, I do. I'll run in and out in a sec. Get out of your hair. I'm sure there's plenty I'm keeping you from too.'

'Such as?'

'Finding something more interesting to put into

those memoirs of yours, bar the history of coffee and beautiful rock formations,' she shot back.

'Not grabbing you?' he asked, his accompanying smile rueful.

Damp curls clung to her cheeks from the ride. She shook them off in frustration. 'Not so much.'

'Hmm. Me neither. Perhaps I'll wait until you come back for all that. Don't want to leave my best stuff in rehearsal.'

They stood facing one another, Hud with his thumbs tucked into the front pockets of his jeans, smiling easily. Kendall gazing into his eyes, her heart racing with a need to get away, to regroup. She needed to think of something else to say and quick or else she might do something stupid like sigh.

She came up with, 'Then maybe you can make a start on cataloguing Fay's things. Or have a better look at that shed.'

'What do you expect me to do with the shed?'

'You're living in a mausoleum. Act like a ghost and that's what you'll become. Move in, Hud. Clean this place up. Open the windows. Let in some light. Or sell the place to someone who'll see it for the beauty it is.'

Her speech came to a halt so that she could take a breath. But it didn't help. His proximity only made her nerves escalate. Her leg ache with trying to stand straight. Her chest squeeze.

He crossed his arms and stared into her eyes.

'The place is yours now, Hud,' she said, her voice thick with aggravation as she did her very best to annoy him too. 'Just do it. Nobody else is going to do it for you.'

His gaze finally disconnected from hers as he glanced deep into the wide open shed swimming with dust and scattered sunshine. He puffed out his chest, stuck out his bottom lip and said, 'You're absolutely right. Maybe I will.'

Kendall's anxiety scattered with her soft laughter. She knew him well enough already to know he would find anything else to do but that. George had been the same. Such a procrastinator she'd told him he ought to win awards for it.

George. His name usually sank to the bottom of her mind like a heavy rock thrown into a pond. But now… *George. George. George.* This time it felt bitter-sweet, and lovely, but ancient. In the past. She remembered Taffy's avowal that if she got out and lived a little, things would be better.

She glanced back at Hud, who was still looking all he-man and proud, as if he really thought he'd have a go at the shed. Not as if the minute she walked away he'd convince himself he had something far better to do with his time. George was in her past. While this complicated, absorbing man loomed so very large in her present.

But as to her future? It still remained a big hazy blur.

'Stay there,' the man of the moment said. 'I'll get your stuff.'

He disappeared into the house and she seriously thought about making a run for it rather than face him. Again. When he returned she took her bags, careful not to brush her fingers against his, knowing his touch would only set off fireworks that seemed to short out the synapses in the good judgement section of her brain.

'I just remembered I have some things to do tomorrow morning,' she said, making things up as she went along. 'Perhaps we should have a day off.'

His expression remained unchanged but she felt the shift in him. The gathering of his thoughts. 'If it's all right with you, I'd really rather not miss a session,' he said. 'Any chance you can come in the afternoon instead? Or the evening? I could put on dinner. Or at least Mrs Jackson in town could deliver something scrumptious.'

She imagined looking at that face across a dining table in some stunning room within Claudel's walls. Fine china. Old silverware. Light glimmering from antique candelabras lining the papered walls... 'Don't worry about dinner. I should be okay by the afternoon. Say four?'

'Four's fine. Until then.' He suddenly took a

long, lazy stride to be at her side. Overwhelming her, filling her vision, her mind, crowding out all other thoughts and feelings until there was nothing but him, his beautiful face, his wide shoulders, his sexy laid-back aura.

Her feet planted firmly on the ground suddenly didn't feel as if they gave her as much protection as she'd thought they could.

He leaned in and kissed her on the cheek, the scent of hot cotton and sandalwood and something indefinably him wafting past her nose, so that she had no choice but to close her eyes and simply drink it in.

Stubble scraped lightly across her cheek, his lips pressed gently against her skin. And then he pulled away. Her eyes fluttered open. His dark hair curled over his ears, tickled the back of his neck and begged to be touched, caressed. It was the kind of hair a woman just wanted to lose her fingers within.

When she dragged her smitten gaze away from his hair to his eyes, to find him watching her watching him, she blabbed, 'You need a haircut.'

His eyes only glimmered all the more. 'I thought I saw a pair of scissors in that pencil case of yours.'

'You saw wrong. And there's a barber in town.'

He blew a raspberry. 'I haven't been to a barber since I was a kid.'

'So how do you…' *look like this?* she was going to say. 'Not have hair halfway down your back?'

'Hunting knife. Pocket knife. A patch was singed when I got too close to a sugar cane burn-off once.'

Of course it had. The guy could have afforded a two hundred dollar haircut in some swanky salon in Melbourne but he was earthy. Rugged. In the line of danger. And she was at once terrified of all that meant while being utterly hooked. All that masculinity and testosterone threatened to make her swoon. To run and not look back. To lean on him. To push him away.

'Excellent,' she said, giving herself a moment to reconnect with the ground again. 'You can tell me all about it tomorrow. People like to know about that kind of stuff.'

'People?'

'Publishers. Readers. Book buyers. TV chat shows. Hair care professionals. You know— *people*. I get the sense you've had some life, Hud. The clothes, the scar—'

She reached out to him then. Unable to help herself. He stood still as a statue as her finger came within centimetres of his top lip. She swallowed hard, trying desperately to fight back the wave of awareness, or perhaps she was trying to fend off such a wave that had come from him.

Either way, she closed her fingers into a ball, let

her hand drop and said, 'The sign of a good story teller is one who doesn't hold back,' then hitched her bag to the other shoulder and stepped away. 'I'll see you tomorrow at four.'

'I'll be here.'

She shot him a quick chummy salute and left, the layers to Hud Bennington's personality tumbling through her mind as if she were flicking fast through the pages of an immense book.

Hud watched Kendall disappear from sight into Fay's lush garden, floored to find she was more of an enigma today than she had been before.

He lifted a hand to run a finger across his lips, trying to secure the feeling of her soft skin against his mouth. The scent of her hair, so warm from a day in the sunshine. And the soft sigh that had escaped her lips as her eyes had fluttered shut.

Then his mobile phone vibrated in his pocket. It hadn't made a peep in days. Though, truth be told, he'd 'forgotten' to turn it on the last two days. He pulled it out and screened the call. It was from Grant, the sound guy from his crew.

This time he hadn't bothered to ring, as the last five times Hud had ignored him. This time he'd left a long text message:

'we leave london thursday week on a new as-signment. northern africa. celebrity adoption story. gorgeous scenery and cute baby photos. cushy. yours if you're up for it. call us! and really really soon…'

He stared at the phone a little while longer, his thumb hovering over the reply button.

His crew were his friends. And, for the past decade, the closest thing to a family he had. And yet here he was treating them as if they didn't matter. As if they were no more to him than the trillion individuals who had flitted in and out of his life as he'd blithely stepped from one airport tarmac to another in search of…what? What having *them* in his life actually already gave him?

Having no contact with them wasn't helping him make up his mind about anything.

So did that mean he truly had something to make up his mind about? Perhaps it was a young man's game. At thirty-two he was hardly middle-aged, but at some point he'd run out of expectations, of hope for questions to be answered.

Or perhaps—and this one was by far the most left field, the most unexpected, the least likely, the craziest, maddest idea, but the one that continued resonating long after he first thought it…

He glanced through the garden to the tops of the pine trees beyond. He had never found one thing, one person, to make him want to stay in one place longer than he had to.

Until now.

It couldn't hurt to stay. For a while longer, at least. What he felt for Kendall was different, deeper, far less easily definable, and far more persuasive compared with what he'd had with Marcie. This place was nothing like London. He was older now. Wiser. Surely he owed it to himself to find out for sure if he had it in him to be that kind of man. Once and for all.

He shifted his thumb a tad to the left and cleared the message from existence.

'So how did it go today with Mr Fabulous?' Taffy asked. 'More exciting stories from the trenches?'

'Yeah,' Kendall said, flopping down backwards on to the big squishy green velvet couch in their lounge room. She pulled a red satin cushion over her face and breathed through it. Then pulled it away to look at Taffy, who appeared to her upside down at the head end of the couch. 'Well, not so much actually.'

'No? I would have thought he'd seen some stuff. Though if you just stick that face on the cover of a book, then stories of land-mines and gunshot wounds and hiding out from guerrilla soldiers for three days on his first Voyager story wouldn't even matter. It'd sell like hotcakes anyway.'

'Land-mines?' Kendall asked, twisting her head so that Taffy's upside down head didn't make her feel like she had vertigo. 'He never said anything about land-mines.' But as she said the word out loud she knew the sudden topsy-turvy feeling in her stomach had nothing to do with Taffy.

'Ooh, yeah. I used to subscribe to *Voyager Magazine* years ago just in case his name appeared below a photograph. The guy has done some crazy things. And you're the lucky one who's getting to hear them first hand.'

'But I had no idea they involved gunshots and land-mines,' Kendall said.

'So what do you guys talk about every day? Run me through today, for instance. Minute by minute breakdown. Don't leave out anything. What he was wearing. What he drank. What he smelt like.'

Sandalwood, Kendall thought, recollecting his scent so clearly he could have been lying right beside her. She breathed in through her nose, suddenly fearing that after their bike ride and their nap on the banks of Saffron Falls that she had carried his scent with her. That Taffy would notice. And wonder about. And decipher. And push. And she'd be forced to dig deep and think honestly and she was scared what she might admit. A sudden headache began at the back of her head and radiated outward.

Kendall looked down at a ragged fingernail. 'He talks shop, I type. Most days we stop to eat at some stage. Something brought to the house by Mrs Jackson. Then I leave, and I swim and I come home. Are you sure about the gunshots and the land-mines?'

'Course I'm sure. The guy's a fearless crusader of the first order. I always thought of him as Indiana Jones meets Ansel Adams. What would I have to gain by…? Oh… I see.'

'You see what?'

'We're not kidding around any more. You are really into this guy.'

'Rubbish.' Kendall sat up so fast her head swam and her vision turned fuzzy around the edges. As she waited for it to clear, she felt Taffy slump into the space her chest had just vacated.

'Rubbish, my sweet patooty. You are crazy about Hud Bennington.'

Kendall closed her eyes and licked her suddenly dry lips. She couldn't be. She shouldn't be. He was beyond gorgeous while she was damaged goods. He was holding something back in the stories he was telling, more than she'd even imagined from what Taffy had just told her. And the idea of getting attached to Claudel made him fidget as if he had fire ants in his shoes. He wanted to go back out there, to jump out of planes and wrestle with snakes and play cops and robbers or whatever it was he really did with his time.

The idea of falling for a man who was leaving town in less than two weeks had been self-destructive enough, but a man so in the path of danger? She'd lost a man she'd loved with her whole being once before. And it had torn her apart.

To fall for Hud and then wave goodbye, and then wait for the news article telling her he'd been killed in some crazy stunt overseas… If she had any remaining sense of self-protection, she would not put herself through that.

She looked in Taffy's eyes, saw nothing but love and took a deep breath and took the plunge into the deep, dark truth.

'I…like him,' she admitted. 'And it's like we are on the same wavelength, or like we've met before. We just kind of…get one another. And it's flattering. And kind of exhilarating. And he makes me laugh. And makes me feel special. And challenged. And wrong, and right, and interested in new things. And sometimes I look up and catch him watching me and my heart just wants to leap through my chest and tug me out of my chair and across the room and into his arms and oh, God, Taffy, what the hell was I thinking in letting things get this far?'

Kendall buried her face in her palms and shook. She just shook. Uncontrollably.

Taffy's hand landed upon her back and began to play with her hair, soothing her until her shakes subsided. 'Exactly how far have you let things get?'

Kendall breathed in deep through her nose and sat back up straight, though her eyes remained tightly shut as she remembered lying on the grass in the thicket watching Hud rest, watching the rise and fall of his chest and the flicker of his thick eyelashes as he drowsed, clenching her fingers so that she would not give in to the aching desire to reach out and brush the stray curls from his forehead.

'Far too far,' she reiterated.

'Have you guys…' Taffy's voice dropped as did her chin '…had sex?'

'No! No. God, no. We haven't even kissed.' Though there had been moments, and plenty of them, where she'd thought it might happen. Where she'd wished she had the requisite amount of guts to follow through on what the look in his eyes said he wanted.

'Right,' Taffy said, her voice rich with sarcasm. 'Well here in the twenty first-century, not having sex with a man you are crazy about after—how many dates have you guys been on now? Five? Is not considered going too far.'

'We haven't had even *one* date.'

'He's made excuses to see you, you've been to his house several times, you've shared meals, you've looked lovingly into one another's eyes… Heck, Kendall, a girl would kill to be afforded such dates. While Jonesy has just offered me a spare ticket to go to see the rodeo with him next month. I'm a sucker while what you have is old-fashioned romance.' After a pause Taffy added, 'Unless…'

'Unless what?'

'Nothing.'

'Unless what, Taff? You can't leave something like that hanging; I may never sleep again.'

Taffy grabbed Kendall's hand and held on tight. 'Unless this is all in your head. Unless this is a one-way street. Unless he isn't feeling it too—'

'I get it, Taffy. Jeez.'

Kendall thought about the preparation he'd put into their picnic. The moments when he'd found an excuse to touch her to get her attention. The time spent at the end of each day stretching longer and longer, as though the two of them were loath to let one another go. Her voice still shook as she said, 'It's not just me.'

'Wow,' Taffy said. 'Well, then, my friend, in for a penny, in for a pound. A man like this isn't going to land himself, you know. You're going to have to tell him.'

'Tell him what, exactly?'

'Tell him you have the hots for him.'

Then what? Kisses? Sex? And *then*? He certainly wasn't the type to settle down and she already had settled down. No matter how resolved Taffy was that she was on the right path, she could see no happy ending.

'Seriously,' Kendall said, pulling her hand away from Taffy's to habitually neaten her skirt. 'The hots? You are stuck in the eighties, my friend.'

'I was a baby in the eighties.'

'Nevertheless, it permeated.'

'Well, permeate this: you like him, he likes you, that's the biggest hurdle gone. The rest is all gravy. Okay?'

Kendall said, 'Okay,' primarily to stop talking. Her little gab sessions with Taffy were only making things more complicated. She dragged her weary limbs off the couch. 'Now, I'm so far behind on my work I have to beg use of the Internet tonight, if that's okay.'

'So we're done with this subject?' Taffy asked.

'So far overdone the edges are burnt.'

'Ooh, but did you find out who the tattoo woman was? She could be the fly in our ointment.'

'Mirabella is what he calls his favourite camera.'

'Ha! Priceless.'

'You mean pointless. If he loves his work enough to brand himself with a needle and ink, it's obvious that's his one great consuming passion.'

'And what's yours?'

Kendall opened her mouth then shut it. For she didn't have one. Life lived on an even keel didn't allow for such exotic pursuits. 'The very second I get one you'll be the first to know,' she said.

Then she grabbed her bag and hobbled upstairs to change into her oversized velour track pants, a loose grey T-shirt and knee-high socks, her comfort outfit she usually saved for fat days and the first of the month blues. Then she came back downstairs and buried herself in her paid work.

Later that night, as she snuggled under her light eiderdown, she gingerly stretched out her left leg, waiting for the pain to pinch but it never came.

Not wanting to push her luck, she slowly tucked herself back into her usual flamingo position on her side, right leg bent, and slowly but surely drifted to sleep, feeling more conflicting emotions, more as if she were being torn in eight different directions than she had in her entire life.

It wasn't until she woke the next morning that she realised in a flash that the day before she'd completely forgotten to take her swim.

CHAPTER EIGHT

HUD didn't actually get to the shed that afternoon
or the next morning. Even though Kendall's words
rang in his ears every moment he lay on the couch
in the library and read, or lazed on the back lawn
with his face turned to the sunshine.

*His house. His life. And nobody could fix either
of them bar him.*

She'd made a fair point. But he wasn't all that
convinced he could fix them either. So instead he
took an easier piece of Kendall's advice and took
a tour of the rest of his house.

In the desk in Aunt Fay's study he found a black
folder with his name on it containing notes written
in Fay's looping hand. Notes about her garden, her
furniture, the code keys to her safety deposit
boxes. Papers that had been ready for him a decade
earlier when he hadn't been ready for them.

He picked up an envelope and a key slipped out.
A car key with a keyring and address on it.

'Well, I'll be blowed.'

Fay's ancient burgundy Bentley. The address was a mechanic in town. He could only hope the place was still there, still living up to the agreement to keep the car serviced and ready to drive the moment he returned. As though Fay had always known he would. One day.

He looked through the top floor window to the front driveway and ran a hand over his mouth. In town. He still hadn't made a trip. Hadn't been to see if his favourite old tree was still standing or had been sacrificed to the gods of progress as he'd found so many things of beauty were.

He did have until four o'clock while his partner in crime ran errands, or washed her hair, taught deaf children how to sign or whatever it was that kept her from him this too long morning.

It took a leisurely half-hour to walk through the pine forest, using the very same route Kendall no doubt took every day, until he found himself on Peach Street.

Stretching his legs felt good. As did the change of scenery. Saffron was extraordinarily pictur-esque. With its row of mature liquid ambers lining the main street, it felt like something out of a New England postcard.

The street looked just the same, as did the shopfronts. Though a few new cracks and patches and signs littered the old.

He soon found himself outside the local newspaper offices, not that he was looking for them, of course. It was simply a good point at which to cross the street. He stopped briefly and peered through the front window but, of the several staff milling about nattering over coffee, none of them was the one he was looking for. Or not looking for. He was just…

Oh, hell. He was looking for her.

Kendall's company invigorated him. Without it there was far too much time to spend with the noise in his head. But she wasn't at work, so he moved on.

As he passed by the post office a waving hand caught his attention. At the other end of the hand was a voluptuous woman with riotous blonde curls and ruddy cheeks. He looked over his shoulder but he was it. So he pulled open the glass door and went inside.

'Howdy, stranger.' The woman's smile grew as did his level of recognition.

'Taffy?'

She grinned and leaned in to offer her cheek for a kiss. He suddenly remembered a time when she would have offered him much more. An early bloomer with early curves, that one had been. Jail bait and all.

She brushed her breast against his chest in a move that was pure habit. For now she had grown into her curves and turned out as pretty as he would have imagined. She was attractive, willing and daring as all get out but not the girl for him.

'Wow, you're all grown up,' he said prudently.

'That's what ten years away from a place will give you, Hud. Change.'

'Tell me about it. So what are you doing here?'

She waved a handful of stamps and a bag of padded envelopes. 'Stationery shopping. The lowly job of the junior receptionist, I'm afraid. The big question of the day is what are you doing here?'

'You waved at me,' he said, crossing his arms and purposely misreading the meaning of her sticky-beak statement.

'Right. So I did,' she said through a grin. 'Do you have time for a coffee?'

'Aren't you heading back to work?'

'A girl needs a tea break at least four or five times a day.'

'Right,' he said, thinking that she was Kendall's friend. Kendall's housemate. This was an opportunity too good to pass up. 'As does a boy, come to think of it. You lead the way to the best coffee shop in town.'

'Don't get your hopes up.'

'Mr Bennington,' a voice called out just as they

reached the door. 'Don't you want your mail while you're here?'

'I have mail? Then bring it on.' He ambled up to the counter. 'Do I need to sign anything?'

The woman, with the name Margo stitched into her pink shirt, blushed. 'Oh, no, I know who you are.'

'Of course you do.'

She handed over a bundle of mail. Hud recognised the letterhead of Voyager Enterprises in London on the top envelope and that was enough for him to lift his T-shirt and slide the mail into the gap at the back of his jeans.

He turned to find Taffy, her beaming smile cute as a button, but not enough to rid him of the tension at the thought of what that letter might entail, especially on the back of yesterday's desperate text message. If he'd turned to find another local, one with luminous blue-grey eyes and dark, silky Botticelli hair, it might have been a different story.

'Shall we?' Taffy said, sliding her hand into the crook of his arm and angling him to a nice-looking café next door. After ordering and collecting their drinks, they found a table on the pavement.

'I was madly in love with you when I was a kid,' Taffy said before he'd even taken a seat.

'Rightio.'

'Oh, now, don't go all panicky and shy on me, Hud. I'm so over you. Many men have crossed my threshold since that time. It took that many to wipe away your memory.' Her voice became all faded and soft as she looked at some point over his shoulder.

Hud shifted uncomfortably on his seat and wondered if it was too late to feign a forgotten dental appointment.

'Kidding!' Taffy said, her eyes shooting back to his, and the relief he felt was immeasurable.

He laughed. 'You had me worried there for a second, kiddo.'

Taffy grinned. 'I've learnt a few tricks since you saw me last. Wanna come home with me so I can show you?'

By this stage Hud had finally found himself in tune with her line of banter. 'Ah, but I wouldn't want you to take ten steps backwards after all your progress in getting me out of your system.'

'Right answer. Now, along those lines, I hear you've got to know my friend Kendall quite well recently.' Taffy sipped on her iced coffee through a straw, but her eyes bored into his.

He felt as though the real reason for her invitation to sit down for coffee had hit with a vengeance, and while he'd been willingly looking the wrong way.

Carefully choosing his words, he said, 'We've become acquainted. Yes. Funny story how too. Did she tell you—?'

'Ooh, yeah. She tells me everything. Has done for years. Best buds we are. Me and Kendall. Almost like sisters.'

Hud smiled and nodded, not quite sure what she was trying to tell him. 'Lucky her,' he said.

'Mmm. Has she told you about how we became friends?'

'Ah, she said she dated your cousin a while back, I believe.'

Taffy's blonde brows took a quick trip skyward. 'She actually told you that? Wonders will never cease. But they didn't just date. She and George were engaged.'

Again Taffy went back to her iced coffee, leaving Hud to deal with the huge well of gaping silence. Kendall, engaged? *Was* engaged. Meaning not now. Somehow that helped quell the sudden uproar in his stomach.

'Well, she's a great girl. That cousin of yours was some kind of clod to have let her go.'

Taffy smiled, his defence of Kendall scoring a hit. But then she said, 'Not quite the way it happened, in fact.'

'No?' Hud said, leaving a gaping well of silence himself this time so that hopefully Taffy would stop dilly-dallying and get to her point, whatever it may be.

'They were high school sweethearts. I can't quite remember the big engagement, but it was just kind of expected they'd get married. I lived with George's family through high school, and Kendall was there almost as much as I was. She finished her English degree at Uni, George had two more years to go on an engineering degree, and then they were planning to marry and travel and generally lead a fabulous life.'

Travel? So that was why she'd never gone overseas. She'd planned to go with…him. 'And then?' he asked, his voice coming out deeper than normal.

Taffy sighed. A great big melodramatic sigh. But behind it all Hud saw real regret, and he suddenly didn't want to know what had happened next.

'George died in a car crash. She was driving. Swerved to avoid a bird or a kangaroo or some-thing. The family never forgave her. She was left out in the cold. In hospital. Alone. I visited when I could but by then I was working full-time back here. A month or so later she checked out, disap-peared off the face of the earth for a few months,' she said behind her hand like the rest of it hadn't been gossip as well. 'Then one day she turned up at my door. I was happy to take her in. She's a sweet kid who deserves far better than life has dished out to her.'

He wished he could turn back the clock and have never asked. That he had not added this to the Kendall York kaleidoscope. It was simply far too...real. His glorious, vibrant distraction had a past. Had hurts of her own.

Taffy shook her head. 'You know we're hardly a small town here. Practically an outer suburb. But it's still the kind of place where generations have settled and stayed. People know one another's business. Many of them had met George from when he visited my family here as a kid. So it took time for Kendall to be accepted.'

Hud ran a hand over his mouth to halt the spray of swear words he felt a sudden need to let forth. 'Yet she stayed.'

Taffy pursed her lips and nodded. 'She stayed, she forged a path, relationships with the locals, and has worked like a trouper, not having taken one day of holiday in three years.'

'But why bother? Why not just start again somewhere new?'

'I have my theories, but really you'd have to ask her.'

He didn't need to ask her. Things just kind of stopped spinning and fell into place. 'She stayed as some sort of penance, didn't she? For running in the first place.' He'd sensed she was brave when they'd first met, but now he knew.

'Wow,' Taffy said. 'What *do* you two talk about when she goes over there every morning?'

'The weather,' Hud said with a subtle smile, 'mostly.'

Taffy grinned. 'Of course you do.' She slurped down the last of her iced coffee. 'Quite something, isn't she?'

Hud's words exactly. Kendall York was something all right. In fact she was a million somethings rolled into one package. She was a good luck charm, an emotional lightning rod, sharp as a tack, faint-hearted only inside her head. And with abundant human flaws and frailties.

'Taffy?' Kendall's voice cut through the conversation.

Hud looked up to find his brave girl casting a shadow over Taffy. Since she was backlit by the bright summer sun he had to shield his eyes to look at her.

She had a small, scruffy-looking dog that looked to be near a hundred dog years old on a lead at her heels. The early summer sunshine shot a dozen different colours through her glorious hair. He couldn't have lit her better if he'd had a studio and a day in which to do it.

'Hi,' he said.

Kendall glanced briefly his way. 'What are you guys doing here?'

'Coffee,' Taffy said, holding up her now empty glass.

'I bumped into Taffy in the post office,' Hud said. 'And after this I'm heading down to pick up Fay's car. I hope the Bentley's been kept at the mechanic's, but I'm not sure what I'll find after all this time.'

'Oh, she's in great nick,' Taffy said. 'The boys take her out for a drive maybe four times a year to keep her running smooth.'

'Good news, then.' He glanced back at Kendall, at her furrowed brow, her stubborn chin, her bemused eyes glaring at Taffy and ignoring him.

This was the first time he'd seen her outside Claudel's grounds, in the real world. Her world. She didn't seem all that thrilled by the notion, while since the moment he'd heard her voice the blood rushing through his veins had heated, quickened, woken his senses far more rapidly than any coffee he'd ever had.

If history told him anything, the things one built up in one's head as being something special would only serve to disappoint in the end. He'd been let down and he'd let others down. He wondered what this woman would have to do to make him think she had wings of wax after all.

'Kendall, darling heart,' Taffy said, shattering the tense silence. 'Sit. I've had my catch-up with your gorgeous friend here. Grab a coffee. And get Hud another. His has gone cold and he barely touched a drop.'

Taffy stood, grabbed her friend by the arm and all but shoved her into her warm chair. But Kendall bounced back up as though her backside was made of rubber. The poor dog stood, then sat, then stood again. 'Can't,' she said. 'Errands, remember.'

Hud stood too, so as not to be left out. Kendall flinched as his chair made a loud scraping noise against the concrete.

Taffy blinked at Kendall, before understanding dawned, bright and phoney. 'Riiiight. Errands. With Orlando in tow. Of course, how could I forget? Well, Hud, my break time is over anyway, so I'll leave you two to say your goodbyes in private.'

She kissed Kendall on the cheek, though it looked as though Kendall wanted to bite her right back, then ran a quick hand over the scruffy dog's ears before flouncing off and leaving Hud and Kendall standing on either side of the small outdoor table.

'I don't mind another coffee if you're up for it,' he said.

She opened her mouth. Closed it. Looked at her watch, then over his shoulder, her eyes flickering

over every person who walked by as though terrified somebody might see her sitting here. With him.

He laughed. It was either that or turn stiff from
tension. 'Kendall, relax.'

'Excuse me?'

'You're making me jumpy. Hell, my right foot
is tapping so hard against the concrete I could
quite easily pull a muscle.'

'Perhaps you've simply had too much coffee
already,' she said, her big blue-grey eyes now
steady upon his face.

Hud laughed again, beaten. 'Perhaps I have.'

But one thing he knew he'd had nowhere near
enough of was her. Deeper layers, and frailties,
and all.

He moved around the table. When she saw what
he was doing she backed up, quickly, the heel of
her boot catching in a crack in the pavement.
Lightning fast, he grabbed her hand and righted
her. The momentum brought her flush against
him, her free hand resting against his chest for
balance, looking up into his eyes.

Her blue pupils were flecked with strands of
quicksilver, mirroring the changeable thoughts
slipping so fast through her mind he couldn't
hope to keep up. Up close her skin was pale and
perfect bar a smattering of tiny freckles across
her nose. And her lips, such luscious lips,

usually on the verge of contradicting him, but right now slightly parted, moist, and more kissable than any two lips he'd set eyes on in his entire life.

She blinked and in that half second seemed to melt ever so slightly against him. Her fingers gripped into the cotton of his T-shirt, scraping against the hairs of his chest.

'Hud,' she said, her breath whispering against his mouth.

'What do you want, Kendall?' he managed.

'I want you…to let me go now.' She leant away from him, eyes wide, chest lifting and falling despite her best efforts to appear cool.

'I don't have to,' he said, his voice low and soft and meant only for her. For now that he finally had her in his arms he couldn't seem to let her go.

She blinked up at him, her hand scrunching harder into the fabric covering his chest.

'I'm not going to fall,' she said, her voice more determined than her actions, which were telling him something quite the opposite.

Maybe what she was really telling him was that she didn't want to fall and, when it came down to it, he didn't want to either. She had gone way past the point of being his muse, or a fun distraction, or an excuse not to do what he'd come to Saffron to do. Now she was…something he'd never experienced before. And that meant she was an unknown entity. A danger. An obstruction.

Yet still he wanted to kiss her. To slide his arms around her heavenly waist, feel her press her curvaceous body against him for real and taste that tempting mouth. To lose himself in her completely, as he so nearly did simply by being in her company.

Maybe then he could rid himself of this need for her. This consuming desire to be with her. To see the world through her eyes rather than his own. This compulsion to put all his eggs in one basket. Again... The same mistake he'd made over and over throughout his life.

He'd been certain during his childhood that the next time his parents would take him with them overseas. It had never happened.

And then he'd put every effort into his career, hoping the constant adventure might be so fantastic he'd understand why leaving him behind had been so easy for his parents in the first place. Yet he'd never found his answer.

And now he looked to her. This woman. Putting so much hope in her was unfair. Especially considering that the day he realised that she wasn't what he'd built her up to be, he would move on again.

He looked down into her eyes as she continued to cling to him despite her protestations that it wasn't what she wanted. If he leaned in and pressed his lips to hers, she wouldn't pull away. He knew it as well as he knew his own weaknesses. So he gathered every ounce of strength he had inside and mentally and physically unwrapped himself from her, letting her go.

'You have a dog,' he said, bending down and scratching the mutt behind the ear until his back leg started to twitch in bliss.

'Umm…' she said, her brilliant eyes still trying to focus. 'This is Orlando. He lives with us. He just turned up one day and never left. Kind of like me, I guess.'

'He's…cute.'

She bent down to scratch behind his other ear. Her head tilted to one side as the dog's big brown eyes looked lovingly up at her. 'He's deaf. He sniffles a lot. And he's the pickiest eater on the planet. But we love him anyway.'

Their scratching hands met. Kendall pulled away as though burned and shot to her feet. Hud followed more slowly.

'Soooo,' he said, 'which way are you heading? I'm going to the mechanic.'

'Right,' she said, straightening her clothes, and her hair, and her story. 'I'm going the complete opposite direction.'

Smart move, Hud thought. 'I'll see you around four, then.'

At which time he would get over himself and talk. Get the impeding thoughts out of his head and on to paper so that he could sell his story, or burn the whole thing in a midnight ritual on the back lawn.

The time had come.

'See you at four.' Kendall gave the lead a light tug, then spun on her heel and took off down Peach Street.

And Hud wondered how on earth they would be able to work together that afternoon and the next, and the next, without him ravaging her the minute she walked through his front door.

CHAPTER NINE

THAT afternoon Hud sat on the couch in the sitting room, running a finger over his bottom lip as he re-read the letter from Voyager Enterprises asking him for an official date of return. It had been two months and one week since he'd been found in an alleyway in Salento, left for dead, clothes torn, weight lost, bloody-lipped.

One month since he'd left the London hospital with his rucksack and camera bag, saved by his crew the night he'd gone missing. And almost a week since he'd been holed up in Claudel, looking to find his way back to the bracing lifestyle he'd worked so hard to have.

He shot to his feet and let the letter drift to the coffee table. He ought to have been on the phone to Voyager in a second.

This place was making him soft. Making him daydream his days away staring at clouds, taking picnics, reading Shakespeare for pleasure, for

God's sake. He needed to end this. This flirtation with the unrealistic fantasy life he was living in this big old house.

But he couldn't call Voyager while he felt like this. He needed to at least seem rational when he made that phone call. He couldn't stay inside and brood either. He needed to clear his head of Colombia two months ago, the backwaters of the big wide world for the foreseeable future, and Kendall York right now.

He stalked to the back door. But this time, for the first time, on the way out he grabbed Mirabella, his trusty camera, out of her damaged canvas bag, sliding the strap over his head and tucking it crossways over his left shoulder.

The weight of her felt…good. Familiar. As if he'd been walking around without his watch for the past two months and it now filled the once naked dent on his left wrist.

He stood on the back step and played with the zoom and focus in one slick move. Instinct took over as if she were an extension of his arm. He pointed the lens at a nearby rose bush lit by a beam of light shooting through the branches of an overhead elm tree. The dark grey-green of the leaves heightened the mixed pinks of the flowers. And, as though it had been waiting for its close-up, a small red bug fluttered out of the sky and landed on a delicate petal.

Hud took a short breath, held it, and depressed the button. The image stayed on the LCD screen. Beautiful. Colourful. Magical.

Encouraged, he walked with the lens to his right eye, left eye open to make sure he didn't run into anything, and waited for something, some impossible frame imbalance, some fantastical ray of light, some image that made an aesthetic impact.

He was almost blinded when a slice of light hit him right through the lens. He swore and lowered the camera to see glimpses of glass through the leaves of heavy undergrowth. The pool house. With all of its canted angles and mixed light and smooth gleaming surfaces and deep dark corners.

'Perfect.'

He pushed his way through the undergrowth and crunched over the dead leaves and patches of pine needles until he found a windowpane with a spot clean enough to shoot through. Then he found a comfortable position leaning against the wall and looked through the glass.

His breath hitched and his every movement ceased when he saw Kendall inside the pool house.

Not gliding serenely through the water as he had seen her that first day. Just sitting on the edge, the dark green sundress she'd been wearing earlier hitched up around her thighs, her pale legs resting in the water, letting the natural buoyancy carry them.

Her hands gripped the edge of the pool, her hair was long and loose down her back and she was looking out into the water.

Before he knew what he was doing, he lifted his camera, right hand and left working in tandem to lock the focus on to her face. The mould creeping in from the edges of the glass created an exquisite frame around her. The shafts of light streaming through the glass roof reflected off the pool and put her lovely profile into perfect relief. The dreamy faraway look in her eyes was mesmerising. Intoxicating.

She shifted then. Hud stilled, just as he had a hundred times before when his secret subject had seemed about to turn his way. In the past such individuals had been villagers hard at work, bad men doing bad things in bad places, even dangerous wildlife seeking out a predator, or prey.

But the thought of this woman catching him made his heart race far harder than it had any of those times. As though the consequences of being discovered watching her covertly would be more far-reaching.

He relaxed very slightly when he saw she was just readjusting her skirt, lifting it around her thighs, revealing…

He instantaneously pulled his eye away from the lens.

But even from that distance he could easily make out snaking scars twisted painfully around her left thigh, finishing just below her knee. Pale scars. Long ago scars. But dreadful-looking all the same.

Her gaze shifted then also. Moving from some faraway point to her leg. She ran a light finger over the bumps and coils of knotted skin, her face twisting. But not from physical pain. It was a pain that tore at Hud's heart. It was a pain fuelled by, of all things, shame.

In that moment everything made so much sense. The long skirts, the dread of trying new things, of new people. Her reticence. The safe job. The safe town. The safe life.

God let things slide the world over? Well, he did the same in pretty Saffron. Kendall had driven the car that had killed her fiancé. She'd been scarred by it emotionally and physically. And now she paid her penance by living out her life tucked away from the bright lights and glory and adventure that she'd wanted in her youth.

She truly had no idea how beautiful she was. How instantly charming. How good people took to her, not because she gave them time but because she couldn't bury who she was. How she might have stopped running but only to go into hiding.

He put the camera back to his eye, drew sharp focus on her face—her engaging, lovely face with its big sad eyes. And his finger depressed the shoot button. The soft clicking sound reminiscent of old style cameras whirred comfortingly in his ear.

He zoomed, he refocused, he shifted angles, changed the frame and just kept clicking.

Finally he zoomed out and shifted focus to her legs, which she had now locked together so that under the shifting dark water they looked like a mermaid's tail. He couldn't help but smile as he took a shot. The image that came back to him on the display hid none of her scars, none of her sadness, and none of her ethereal beauty.

It had to be one of the best photographs he had ever taken. The colour, the light and the emotion were rich and intimate and leapt out of the screen. And, in that instant, he felt as though a part of him that had been missing for all too long had returned.

'Trust you to be looking for the hard way to do everything,' he said softly.

He watched her for a few more moments as the bitter reality before him reminded him why he needed to get on a plane back to London and to move on with his life.

It was time he stopped hiding too.

* * *

Kendall sat with her feet dipped into the pool, staring out into the dark shifting depths.

Well, she kind of pretended to stare into them. Really her mind was filled with the image of Hud Bennington. In town. Clean-shaven for the first time since she'd met him. Dressed in neat and tidy clothes. Smiling and chatting and looking so at ease, so at home in Saffron, as though he'd never moved away. As though he belonged.

She knew it was dangerous allowing herself to think that way. He had moved away but, by the drop cloths still covering half the furniture in his house, he hadn't really moved back. She knew in her heart of hearts he'd be here another week, if she was lucky.

Only now the danger of losing him wasn't enough to turn her away. She'd quite simply never met anyone who affected her like he did. As suddenly. As intensely. As physically. She felt it tingling in the tips of her fingers. Burning like a whisper of smoke in the back of her head. Squeezing her lungs. Weakening the tendons in the backs of her knees.

And that afternoon, as he'd held her hand and her gaze for a few long glorious moments on the cracked Peach Street pavement, he'd also held her heart.

She knew she oughtn't to be influenced by

strumming harps and arrows shot from little fat flying cherubs from the heavens. Life was messy. Happily ever afters weren't there for the taking. Hud was searching for something too, and the chances of that something being a somewhat steady, small town girl with a limp and a past were about a gazillion to one.

But she loved him.

She knew it to be true because she'd loved once before. A sweet, shy, smart kid who'd worshipped the ground she walked on, and then in the blink of an eye was gone, taking with him the life she knew. Now she loved again. A tough, confident, experienced man who lived dangerously, kept his feelings close to his chest and made her feel like a warrior princess. As if she could be anything. Do anything.

It was nearing four o'clock so she would have to get moving soon. She pulled her prune-like feet from the water, stood on shaky legs, let her long dress drop to ankle length and gathered every ounce of strength she had in her bones to go and find Hud.

Wondering all the while if that can-do feeling he instilled in her might include being able to make him love her back.

The scrape of Doc Marten boots on the wooden floor told Hud that Kendall had arrived. He heard her let her bag fall to the floor beside the desk before ambling further inside the sitting room.

Feeling overwhelmed by what he was about to do, by way of hello he merely held out the book in his hand towards her, title page out. 'I've been reading your friend Will Shakespeare.'

'Wow,' she finally said. 'I don't know what to say. Apart from the fact that I get a gold star from the Shakespeare lovers of the world for converting another to the cause.'

'Hmm,' Hud said. 'It's taken me a bit but I think I'm starting to understand him a tad more. I thought this passage notable. Listen:

"A good leg will fall; a straight back will stoop; a black beard will turn white; a curl'd pate will grow bald; a fair face will wither; a full eye will wax hollow; but a good heart, Kate, is the sun and the moon; or rather the sun and not the moon; for it shines bright and never changes, but keeps his course truly."'

He looked up, wondering if she'd have any clue what he was trying to say. That he was trying to tell her he knew.

Her arms were hanging by her sides, her eyes smiling. She had no idea.

'The proposal scene from *Henry V*. I don't quite

know what to say.' She even took a few steps
closer, until she perched against the arm rest of the
couch on which he sat. Her hair hung like a curtain
across half her face as she leant in and looked over
his shoulder at the book.

He caught a waft of pine, of chlorine, and of
something sweet like fruit-flavoured perfume.

She asked, 'Is this where I'm meant to say that
passage at least gives you hope you won't end up
a sad old bachelor looking back on your glory
days when you were young and handsome?'

'You think me handsome?' he asked, half
turning on the chair to face her all the better. This
wasn't going exactly how he'd meant but it had
taken a turn he wasn't arguing with.

Her mouth twisted, as though she was trying
not to smile. 'I think the passage would serve you
better if I could be sure you had a good heart.
Otherwise you're in a lot of trouble.'

'Right,' he said. Then he held a hand to his left
upper chest region. 'I think my heart was actually
hurt by that statement.'

'Well, at least we now know you have one. How
we figure out if it is any good is another matter.'

She smiled then, despite her best efforts not to.
Her eyes shone. Her cheeks were round and pink.
The dark forest green of her sleeveless dress played
perfectly against the rich red wine colour of her hair.

She was beautiful. And her expression was more open than it had ever been. It told him she was so clearly taken with him and it only made his attraction to her quadruple in one beat of his heart.

But she knew so little about him. Just as before that day he'd known so little about her. Her scars were hidden behind her verve and long skirts and layer upon layer of self-protection. Which he was about to peel away as if he were ripping off a Band-Aid.

'I took Mirabella out for a spin earlier today,' he said. 'For the first time in a really long time.'

Her eyes opened wide, unsuspecting. 'Why such a really long time?'

'Colombia,' he said, his mouth suddenly too dry to speak.

She simply nodded. Understanding instinctively even if she didn't know the details. Yet.

'I did a walk around the garden and ended up at the pool house.'

'The pool house,' she repeated, her voice suddenly flat. Wary. 'When was that?'

'About an hour ago.'

Her face lost colour which, considering she was pale enough to begin with was a daunting sight. But, now he'd started this, he couldn't stop.

'I saw you Kendall. Legs in the water, thoughts a million miles away.'

'Why didn't you come inside?' she asked. Her arms slid up to cross across her stomach. 'My being there didn't stop you that first time.'

'You seemed…far away. Like you wanted to be alone. I didn't want to disturb you.'

'Bull,' she said, the ferocity in her voice so strong Hud actually flinched. 'You saw more than that.'

He blinked up at her, suddenly finding himself at the deep end of a dark pool of reed infested water himself.

'I'm not an idiot Hud. The passage you just read out—"*a good leg will fall*".' She lifted a hand to cover her eyes. 'Oh, God.'

'Kendall, I don't think you're an idiot. I wanted to tell you, badly as per usual, how little any of that matters. Sitting on the edge of that pool, you seemed so content, so wistful. You have no idea how envious I was. I only wished I had it in me to feel like that. Like you.'

He reached out to her. She slid off the chair and took two steps backward, away from him.

'Don't even try, Hud. My leg is scarred. Disfigured. In pretty much constant discomfort. While you just sat there and let me open my big mouth and call you handsome.'

'Well, how's this, then? I think you are gorgeous. Completely and utterly bewitching. And you can't tell me you haven't felt it from me.

Haven't felt how much I want to touch you, and kiss you, and be with you every minute I can.'

She shut her eyes tight and shook her head, those words seeming harder for her to hear than that he'd seen her scars.

'Well, it's true.' he said. 'But it's not only that I am so enamoured with you it is a physical strain not to be holding you right now. You're also the one who gave me the urge to get Mirabella out again. I couldn't have done that a week ago. Not until I met you.'

'So what? I seem to have got over myself, so maybe you can too,' she said with such coolness in her voice.

Feeling as if he were on a verbal ice rink in bare feet, he stepped carefully. 'Well, yes, actually. You inspire me in more ways than you can imagine.'

Kendall scoffed, shook her head and picked up her unpacked bag with lightning-quick speed, and then turned and walked away. She practically ran. But not as fast as she would have if she'd had full use of both legs.

The moment she was out of his sight, the room felt cool, empty, devoid of life. It took him less than a second to decide to run after her.

'Kendall,' he said, reaching her just outside the door leading to the garden. He easily passed her and turned to jog backwards. 'Look, there is no need to do this. Don't be such a stubborn fool. Stay. Talk to me.'

Her stormy gaze remained dead ahead. 'Tell me one moment I have ever given you the idea that I would want to open up to you.'

'I'm a good listener. I promise. And it's the least I can do after all the tedious claptrap you've had to listen to from my end.'

'You want me to share, Hud? To talk? To you…the most choked-up raconteur I've ever had the displeasure to meet. For that hardship I deserve far greater compensation than mere reciprocation.'

At least she'd used his name and hadn't called him Jackass or any such reasonable term. He latched on to that one small ray of hope and kept jogging, glancing over his shoulder to avoid nasty fall-inducing obstacles.

'Fine. I'll write you a cheque to cover the emotional distress. Name your price, it's yours. The pool, the car, the house, my soul.'

That one earned him a withering glare for his efforts.

They hit the edge of the garden and glancing didn't do it any more. Something caught against Hud's left heel and, though he reached out for something to break his fall, all he could get a handle on was the skinny branch of a nearby rose bush.

When he hit the ground, backside first, he wasn't

sure which hurt more, the thorn scratches on his palms, his jarred backside or his battered ego.

He sat, head bowed, and gave himself a few moments to catch his breath, realising the fight was lost. Against Kendall York that was almost a given. She was as stubborn as he was blinkered. As willful as he was wayward. Like a south pole to his north. Which was why they were so effortlessly drawn together.

And then a small pale hand reached down into the centre of his vision.

He glanced up, finding Kendall haloed by the afternoon sun behind her, looking like an angel. But he had long since come to the conclusion that she was no angel, no nymph, and no mermaid either.

Kendall York was all too human. Which made his fierce attraction to her all the more consuming. And vulnerable. And terrifying. This place wasn't making him soft—nowhere near as much as being around her was.

None of this could possibly end well.

'I'm bleeding,' he said, showing her his palm, trying to reject her help. After all he was meant to be big and strong. She was meant to be frail and damaged.

'I can see that,' she shot back, flexing her fingers and brooking no argument.

So he took her hand, his calluses rasping against

her smoothness, his large hand wrapping itself around hers and then some. He pushed off the ground as she pulled. He let go to brush himself off. She stood back to shift her heavy bag to a more comfortable position on her shoulder.

'Come on,' she said. 'Get inside so I don't have your death of gangrene on my conscience.' She turned and walked away, the limp in her left leg plain as the light of day. He wondered how he'd never really noticed it before. He who was *all about the visuals*.

Probably because from the second he'd landed there he'd been living a fantasy wrapped in the safe, lovely memories of his youth and had projected said fantasy on to this house, this place, this woman. But fantasies didn't last. Real life always found a way to intercede.

He followed, wondering how to make this venture end with as little bloodshed as possible. He looked down at his bleeding palm and wondered if it was far too late for all that.

CHAPTER TEN

Hud sat on the wooden kitchen bench.

He'd managed to track down yellowed gauze, dark purple antiseptic that was about eight years out of date and a box of bandages which had made him smile when he remembered Fay first buying them, saying now she had a boy in the house she'd need them.

But Kendall had no intention of smiling. She still felt bruised. Confused. And sideswiped. Hud had been out and about with Mirabella again, meaning he was feeling back to his hale and hearty self. Meaning his time here was coming to an end.

And he'd seen her in the pool house, seen her scars, meaning he now knew that she was far from fighting fit. Far from the kind of vigorous go-getting woman he would want in his life.

Her whole world had flipped, and flipped again, and she was back to being poor little Kendall York once more. The girl people had patted on the head when her mother had died. The young woman people had whispered about when her fiancé had died. And she felt so close to bawling her eyes out it was as though she had lost someone near and dear to her all over again.

Only this time she knew that person was her. The woman she had secretly harboured hopes of yet becoming. The woman who was beginning to come out of her shell, to risk and dare to dream, had faded into a figment the moment she'd realised Hud had been quoting a Shakespearean version of *beauty is only skin-deep*.

'Hold out your hand, palm up,' she demanded of him. He did as he was told and she tugged his hand closer, then ran her finger over the trail of the longest scratch, which ran the length of his life line and was definitely more than skin-deep. 'It would take very little for me to hurt you, you know.'

'I'm well aware of that, Kendall.'

At the soft, hazy tone in his voice, she couldn't help but glance up, meeting his beautiful hazel eyes for the first time since she'd run, and her breath suddenly felt as if it couldn't remember where it was meant to go.

He was looking at her…differently. She searched for sympathy. For some kind of *poor you* reaction. But there was none of that. There was only…

Admiration. Respect. A measure of uncertainty. And a good dash of blatant sexual attraction. Unmistakable, even for a girl who hadn't been in such a position all that many times in her young life. But with every stroke of her finger along his palm, the skin at the edges of his eyes contracted, the tendons in his neck clenched, his eyes grew darker and darker. And she just knew.

She tried desperately to find a way to make herself believe that was as bad as pity. Because in that moment it felt far too good. Good in the way it made the skin on the back of her neck warm. Good in the way her knees seemed to melt and her limbs went beautifully lax. Good in the way that her fingers couldn't help but curl around his.

He breathed in deep through his teeth. She looked down to find her fingers were indeed pressed too hard into his wounds. She shook her head and bit her lip to try to negate the sudden rush of heat to her cheeks.

'I warned you, Hud. Stop fidgeting,' she said, as she turned away, switched on the tap and wet some gauze.

'Whatever you say, boss.'

She was smart enough not to look up again as she cleaned his wounds. Though the feel of those large, creative hands under her careful ministrations, the shift and strength of those powerful thighs just below her elbows and the intoxicating scent of his skin were all almost as hard to ignore as the truth in his eyes.

And the memory of his words. Calling her gorgeous. Bewitching. Telling her how much he wanted to kiss her. To hold her. To be with her.

She turned off the tap and unscrewed the lid of the antiseptic when he said, 'So tell me about your leg.'

She ignored him.

'The scars. The limp. And George,' he said without any hint of remorse that he was cutting far deeper than she ever could. 'How did it happen?'

'What the hell do you know about George?'

'Taffy mentioned him in passing yesterday.'

Kendall laughed through her nose, though there was no humour in it. 'Of course she did. I could really strangle both of you right now. And there are plenty of dark, hidden places in the pine forest where I could leave you both to rot.'

'Kendall—'

'I'm just a small town girl with small town stories. Tedious wouldn't even begin to cover it, you don't really want to know and I don't really want to talk about it.'

'I do want to know, and it'll be good for you. To talk. To let someone else in. To share.'

She poured a measure of the dark purple liquid on to a patch of fresh gauze and drowned the poor thing. With a soft curse she threw it into the sink and tried again.

'This from the guy whose face turns white as a sheet at the mention of Colombia but won't tell me why,' she said under her breath. 'This from the guy who mentioned the name of *one* guy he worked with only when pressed. Sharing? I wonder if that fancy boarding school of yours taught you what the word really means.'

'Kendall—'

She dabbed the damp gauze against his cuts, shutting him up. But still more gently than she really wanted to at that moment, especially when she felt the story she didn't want him to know welling on to the tip of her tongue.

'We were engaged,' she said. 'And he died. I was injured in the same accident. Happy?'

'Not overly. Tell me about George. Tell me about you with George.' His hand closed over hers, locking her fingers and the wet gauze within his gentle yet insistent grip.

How could she tell this man about George? This man, whose every touch slithered through her like some new kind of heretofore unknown pleasure. Whose every look branded her. This man, who had captured her attention, and her imagination, and the heart she'd promised she would never give away ever again—about the sweet, easy, comforting love she'd felt for George?

He slid his hand over her wrist, turning her arm to trail his fingers along the soft skin inside. 'It's okay,' he said, his voice a deep hum that washed over her, infusing her with warmth and making her feel infinitely safe. Cocooned in his strength.

'I was impulsive when I was young,' she began. 'Impetuous. Away with the fairies most of the time. Until I met George. Smart, focused, with a huge family. He hated reading.' She'd opened the floodgates the memories swarmed over her like a tidal wave. 'Unless it was a textbook or about the history of bridges or anything equally dry. Never liked museums or art galleries. Poetry made him cringe. But he loved me.'

Hud tugged once and pulled her deeper into the gap between his thighs. He reached out and ran a hand over her hair, his fingers sliding between the waves, running down her scalp. Her eyes fluttered closed and she just let him.

'Then one day,' she continued, 'we were heading up here to visit Taffy on our way to a weekend in Sydney to celebrate my graduation. I was driving, singing ridiculously loud to a song on the radio to annoy him. A fox ran out on to the road. A stupid fox. I swerved. We hit a tree.' Her mouth was suddenly so dry she took a moment to swallow. 'He was killed instantly. A small trail of blood ran down his forehead. Apart from that he looked like he was sleeping. But I knew.'

'Oh, sweetheart,' Hud said, but Kendall was on a roll. She was too far gone, locked into the memory that had haunted her for years. Daily. Then nightly. Then less and less often until she sometimes realised she had gone days without re-membering, and then the guilt that she had survived and he had not almost tore her apart.

'My leg was viced. The pain… God, I can't even hope to describe the pain. But it was not enough to make me pass out. I had to stay there. Screaming. Calling out. Trying to dislodge myself to be able to reach for my mobile phone in my bag on the back seat.'

She felt the tears pouring down her face then. Hot, free-flowing, pooling at the corners of her down-turned mouth.

'And I was in the car, with him, beside me but gone, for three hours before someone found us and sent for help and the Jaws of Life were able to get us out.'

Hud swore, his mouth so close to her ear she felt the waft of his breath tickle against her skin. And she was pulled back from imagining herself sitting in the driver's seat, her head tilted as far to the left as it could be to watch George. To never let him out of her sight. Even though she knew he was gone.

Hud's thumb stroked away her tears, so gently so tenderly that she felt the resultant calm slide down her body until the hum settled in her stomach, warm and unclouded.

'And your leg?' he asked, his voice ragged, as if he were talking through a throat full of razor blades.

'My thigh was pierced by a great hunk of metal, muscles severed. Repaired in ground-breaking surgery. I was the toast of the emergency ward.'

'But it never really healed.'

'Healing is never as simple as medicine and rest,' she said, remembering the kind words of the nurses who couldn't possibly have been as clueless as they had seemed, believing their platitudes to be of some help. Though at the time she'd smiled and thanked them and made them feel better while inside she'd shut down.

'Diet and exercise, they say too,' Hud said. 'All rubbish, if you ask me.'

'And don't forget…give it time,' she added, stunned to find a wry smile tugging at the corner of her mouth. 'I itched to ask them how much time. A month? A year? A day I could circle on my calendar and look forward to, knowing it would all be better then?'

Hud leaned forward and placed a soft kiss upon her hair. And every sense came back online to remind her where she now was, and with whom. She was tucked between his thighs, his hand cupping her cheek, her face warm with tears. She was completely exposed, far more so than when she'd found out he'd seen her ugly scars.

'It wasn't your fault,' he said.

'I know,' she said, gently trying to extricate herself. But he looked deep into her eyes and she couldn't move. Couldn't breathe.

'It wasn't your fault,' he repeated.

'I know,' she repeated after a pause.

He looked into her left eye, then her right, looking so deep inside her she felt it in every nerve-ending, every blood vessel, every cell—the push and pull and tug of history and of him. Here with her right now.

This man, who affected her to her very core. This beautiful, whole, wealthy, healthy, adventurous, go-getting, world-travelled, experienced, giant of a man. This man who she just knew, despite her best efforts to drag herself kicking and screaming from the possibility, she had fallen so completely in love with.

She was so physically attracted to him she feared she couldn't keep it out of her face. She was so emotionally connected to him that every word out of his mouth made her feel as if she had lived his experiences herself.

But she couldn't *have* him. Despite the minute chance she'd given herself in the pool house, she didn't have the practice, or the craft, or the bag of tricks to cope with someone like him. She knew herself well enough to know she would crumble long before he did. So it was simply better to keep herself intact, better to avoid the pain of losing him—to his real passions, and to the world.

And, though she'd told him, and Taffy, and the shrinks, and the doctors and anyone else who asked and pushed and prodded that she knew it hadn't been her fault, she knew that in a way it had been. And Hud only proved it. Loving him was her ultimate penalty. So naturally he wasn't done messing with her just yet.

He tucked his undamaged hand along the back of her neck, deep within her waves, the warmth of his skin soaking into hers until she just wanted to cry a whole lot more. 'Kendall, look at me.'

She did as she was told.

'Your mum isn't going to disappear from your life if you don't write down every detail about her. And neither is George. It's okay to put things in the past. It's okay to look to the future. And it's certainly okay to enjoy things in the here and now.'

'But how can you stop letting it all mean so much?' she asked.

The right corner of his mouth lifted, drawing her eyes downward to curves and perfect planes and tempting lips. 'Questioning your every move, wondering which moment you could have changed to have made it all turn out different? Wondering if you really want your life to be different? Wondering if you could make it more different or if that would be a slap in the face to the ones you left behind?'

Through the clearing blur she looked into his eyes. The left with more gold than the right. She wondered if she looked hard enough she could see through the labyrinthine intellect and layers of self-protection to get a glimpse into his truth as well.

She merely nodded.

'If you ever stumble upon the answer to that one, Ms York, you be sure to let me know. Then we can become quizillionaires together.' His deep voice filled the last remaining empty spaces inside of her.

Whether it was the understanding in his eyes, the gentle ache his touch was pouring through her, or the word *together* that made her do it… Kendall simply stopped thinking, stopped trying to make sense, and be good, and assuage her guilt, and torture herself with what-ifs and simply gave in, leaned in and touched her lips to his.

And Hud's lips… Oh, his lips were like velvet. Hot, sweet, heavenly velvet. They instantly slid and shifted to fit perfectly beneath hers as though he'd only been waiting for this chance.

He used his other hand against her back to draw her in until she was folded completely in his embrace. Her head tilted back as far as it could to give him access to all he wanted, all he needed.

His hands cradling her face, he slid off the counter until their bodies were meshed together. And the kiss deepened. It grew and changed and took on a life far bigger than either of them.

Hud opened his mouth, sliding his tongue between her teeth, encouraging her to give more, to open herself up to him completely. She did just that.

With a soft sigh she slid her arms around his neck. He tasted hot and spicy. Better than she could have imagined. Delicious. And completely inevitable.

She had felt a connection from the moment they'd met. A sameness. As though both of them were somehow coming from the same place. She'd known their only two options were to continue to clash against one another until they broke or to simply keep moving forward until they passed one another by.

But now, in his arms, tasting him, against him, around him, all she could feel were the differences. The hardness of his chest muscles against her breasts. The rigid tendons in his neck beneath her small fingers. The light sandpaper feel of his jaw rasping erotically against her smooth lips.

He was all man. All hard planes and strength and knowledge and maturity and hormones and she was gripped in the throes of wanting more, of wanting to give herself up to her most pure feminine side and drown in it all.

Finally they came up for air as one. Their heavy breathing loud on the quiet afternoon air.

Kendall closed her eyes and leant her forehead against his chest, far, far too moved to look him in the eye.

It wasn't as though she was sweet twenty-three and never been kissed. When she'd checked out of hospital she'd moved to the other side of Melbourne. Had gone out. Every night. Meeting men. Needing the noise, the human contact, to drown out the noises in her head.

But a kiss with feeling. A kiss with connection. A kiss with history and possibility. That was something so very different. So much more. Deeper. More pure. A kiss like that changed a person. Changed a relationship. And there was no going back.

'You can't be cold,' Hud said after a shiver rocked Kendall's whole body.

'Not,' she said. 'Just…shaky.'

'Mmm, I'll take that as a compliment.'

She smiled, the feeling warming her from the inside out and taking a small measure off the edge of her dread.

'Here,' he said, turning her in his arms and lifting her on to the bench, making her feel as light as a feather rather than an average-sized woman.

She braced her hands against the bench when he instantly began to rain perfect hot kisses across her cheek, along her chin, down her aching throat.

Out of control can't always be a bad thing, she told herself as the shift and slide of her hair tickled her bare forearms. Her chest lifted to take in more breaths and at the same time to press closer to him. As though his warmth and energy were the only things keeping her going.

His hand slid gently along her thigh, creating warm waves of pleasure from the point of contact to the rest of her body. He kept pushing, gathering mounds of fabric in its wake. Instinct had her placing her hand over his and easing the fabric back to cover herself up.

But she should have known he wouldn't be so easily deterred. He deftly twisted her hand upside down until his fingers wound around hers and then together they lifted her skirt.

First her ankles felt the kiss of fresh air and

then her calves. As the cotton pulled over her knees she was glad to be sitting, for her limbs simply gave way through a mixture of intense pleasure and ancient fear. Fear of discovery. Fear of being thought lesser. Fear of being blameworthy. Of losing that look in his eye which made her feel beautiful.

He then used both hands to push the fabric over her thighs. Heat pooled at the juncture between them. So close to him, open to him, but achingly void of his direct touch, her breath shot from her lungs in a long juddering sigh.

He pulled away, barely, but enough to look into her eyes. And tell her that he had pushed her as far as he was going to. Anything further would be up to her.

His long fingers rested gently in the folds of her cotton skirt. The scars on her left leg were exposed, white and uneven and obvious and ugly. She felt so vulnerable and yet so luscious, she could barely see straight. But what she could see was enough.

Beautiful hazel eyes. Dark eyelashes. Dark curling hair. The swarthy skin of an outdoorsman. And a fresh scar slicing from his upper lip to the edge of his nostril. Evidence of violence marring his perfection—another connection.

She reached up and ran a finger over the scar.

He flinched. She glanced back at his eyes, knowing if she saw them closing down, pulling away, that this crazy beautiful moment in time would all be over. But he breathed in deep, centred himself and continued to let her do as she needed to do.

Strengthened, Kendall looked back down at his scar. A neat slice. The mark of a knife. Or a piece of glass. Or a fast closed fist. Healed naturally with no modern medicine involved.

She could have asked how it had happened but, after all she had revealed to him, if he dodged her question, or made some kind of joke or distracted her with pretty words as he always had, this heady power surging through her would crumble.

Instead she leaned in and replaced her finger with her mouth, sliding her lips over the spot, the hair of his fresh stubble scratching her soft, overripe skin.

Hud soon gave in and kissed back. And it was a kiss filled with such sweetness, such affection. She stopped thinking over every millisecond, as though hoping to later make notes in her red notebook, and simply gave in to the experience and let his tenderness wash over her like a warm healing shower.

Eons later, Hud cradled her face in one hand and kissed her lingeringly one last time.

Then he looked down at her leg.

CHAPTER ELEVEN

'DOES it hurt?' Hud asked.

Kendall thought about lying, about sticking out her chin and feigning superhuman strength. But the past twenty minutes had been the most honest of her life. 'Not always,' she said. 'Not now.'

'But after you've been standing for too long…'

'Sitting too long, walking too long. But swimming helps.'

'Of course it does.' His beautiful mouth creased into a sweet smile as she finally gave him the real reason behind her desire for his pool.

He then rolled up the arm of his shirt to reveal a long-healed scar slicing vertically up his inner arm. He brought her hand to it, running her fingers along the raised skin, past sinew and dark masculine hair and thick roping veins.

'What happened?' she asked, her voice a ragged whisper as her heightened awareness of him mixed with the imagined horror of what had happened to him while in some scary place working overseas.

'Fell through a plate glass window when I was eight.'

She glanced up at his face and knew he wasn't kidding. 'Here?'

He shook his head. 'Boarding school. I was a tad rambunctious even then. But wait. There's more.'

He leant over and rolled up his right jeans leg, revealing a smattering of grazed skin above his manly left ankle.

'Ouch,' she said, leaning in for a better look, wondering which dangerous far-away place had caused so much damage to such an otherwise perfectly healthy-looking ankle.

'Back streets of suburban London,' he said. 'Motorbike accident when I was your age. Pieces of gravel still make their way out every now and then.'

She looked Hud in the eye, a smile tugging at her cheeks. 'You're a klutz, aren't you, Hud Bennington.'

He rolled his jeans back down and grinned at her. 'I'd like to think of it as having a bold spirit.'

She grinned back, liking this game for several reasons. She was playing it with him. He wasn't feeling sorry for her or repulsed by her scars as he'd seen worse. And so far all of his had come from being a big kid, *not* from shark bites, or knife fights, or being caught in the midst of danger. Taffy's talk of gunshots and land-mines appeared to be another reason to strangle the girl and leave her in a shallow grave.

Her poor wide-open heart eased tenfold.

'Right. Any more?' she asked, allowing her eyes to rove over large patches of skin covered by layers of clothing.

When she looked back into his eyes they were locked on hers and she couldn't look away for the life of her. The ease she had been feeling dissipated and she simply felt airless.

Without blinking, without smiling, he took hold of the bottom of his T-shirt and began to roll the hem upward. Inching the grey cotton slowly, slowly, so that in her peripheral vision Kendall was exposed to a hint of cotton boxers peeking out from beneath low-slung jeans, sculpted curves of tanned skin and stomach muscles the likes of which would take a million sit-ups to achieve and an arrow of dark hair narrowing as it dived beneath his pants.

Which if they had been swimming wouldn't have meant a thing. But like this, alone in his kitchen, after all they had just been through, it felt far more intimate, far more daring. A flash of skin was like a secret revealed. An intimacy shared. A step closer to finding a middle ground.

'What exactly are you trying to show me here, Hud?' she asked, her voice husky.

'Wait for it,' he said, still not breaking eye contact.

'This better be something.'

His eyes creased into a smile and he stopped rolling cotton and looked down. 'There it is.'

Kendall blinked furiously to wet her dry eyes. Then followed the line of his sight to find herself face to face with washboard abs, dark hair, broad chest. So much skin, hot male skin. Hud's skin. She ached to reach out and touch, to run her fingers over all that lovely skin as she had over his arm. His finger ran back and forth across a small red scar between two ribs.

'What's that?' she asked. 'Lose a fight with a protractor in grade school?'

He shook his head. 'I was impaled on an old fence post in an abandoned farm in Kenya. Two years ago. It missed every vital organ but I lost so much blood I passed out. The klutz struck again.'

He was making a joke. But something in the shift of the tone in his voice rattled Kendall. Suddenly this game wasn't fun any more.

The scar on his lip was recent too. The darkness in his eyes, soul deep. The life he led was an enigma to her. The time had come for her to stop shielding herself and to know more. To know everything. To discover how truly ready she was to take on another person's frailties and excesses into her life. To see if she was truly ready to take the second chance at life she'd been given.

'Have you ever been shot?' she asked.

He shook his head. 'No. Thank God.'

Kendall's breath shot from her lungs in a wave of pure relief.

Until Hud continued. 'Though my camera case has. Three holes, to be precise. Guatemala. El Salvador. And Texas. Mirabella was only grazed herself just the once. A small scrape down the side. Mirabella has saved me on more occasions than I care to count.'

Drawing breath in was more difficult again. He was trying to open up, to share, to make her feel as if she wasn't the only one with scars, but all those nasty scrapes did was remind her that, while she one day hoped to see the Eiffel Tower, the man before her lived a life out of a boys' own adventure novel.

She wore sunscreen every day. She didn't drive a car. She held on tight—to her home, her job, facts, her best friend, her community. While she was Miss Feet Firm on the Ground, he threw caution to the wind and looked death in the eye five days out of ten.

And she had fallen for him. In a big way. Hook, line and sinker. The one man in the world who would be least likely to fit into her life. And whose life she would be least likely to have the emotional strength to take on.

For two such people to bend and change and give in so much to meet somewhere in the middle was an impossibility. All that lay ahead of them was heartache. Loss. Goodbyes. Promises that neither of them would have a hope in hell of keeping.

'So when do you go back?' she asked, dreading the answer but at the same time hoping it might put her out of her misery quickly and humanely.

'Where?'

'Over there. Wherever. To the world of gunshots and fence postings with a grudge and long trips and your real life.'

He reached out and slid his hand along her cheek, tucking a curl behind her ear. 'They've sent me a letter asking me just that question. And text messaged me. I wouldn't be surprised if a courier pigeon arrived on my doorstep any day. They have an assignment they want me to participate in.'

'Where?'

'North Africa.'

'When?'

'Next week.'

'So when do you—' She had to stop to swallow as her voice sounded as if she were speaking through sawdust. 'When do you have to decide?'

'If it's up to Voyager, tomorrow wouldn't be soon enough.'

That wasn't an answer. She knew it and, by the shift in his eyes, he knew it too. 'And your book? Does that have to be completed first?'

His eyes crinkled at the corners as he thought before speaking. 'They would prefer it if the story had been told, yes. But I get the feeling they are now in the *all it takes is time* frame of mind.'

'Right,' she said, pushing against his chest and sliding back down on to the kitchen floor. Her dress dropped to cover her up once again. She stood looking up into his eyes and did her best to hide the hurt. He was leaving. He was really and truly leaving. Which, she reminded herself, was far better than being the one they'd call to say he'd been killed on assignment. She couldn't be that person in a million years.

'Why don't we do as we were meant to do and get back into the sitting room and get it done?' she said. 'That way you can make the decision without strings attached, things left undone. No pressure.'

'That sounds like a plan,' he said.

She smiled, patted his chest as though they hadn't just been wrapped in one another's embrace, as though she hadn't spilled her heart to him. As though that same heart wasn't splintering in her chest right that second.

This way he could still leave, a whistle in his step as he finished his sabbatical and headed back off into the wild blue yonder. At least this way one of them would go on their merry way unchanged. Unmarked. No more damage to add to the package.

She slid past him and took her bag back into the sitting room and waited, hoping he wouldn't give her another session about travel visas and customs issues. That at least, before he left, he respected her enough to give her the real story.

Hud had meant to end it. He'd meant to ask the hard questions and make her think it was her decision to pull away. But then she'd gone and, well, been herself. She'd been strong and honest and he'd been undone.

And when those lips of hers had found his—sweet, gentle and provocative—he'd sabotaged his own ends within a split second.

Now she had gone all quietly confident on him. All common sense and decisiveness. All stubborn nervelessness. He knew it was a measure of self-protection, but it was also as sexy as hell.

No pressure? Rubbish. He felt the pressure building inside him as though it was coming from everywhere. Voyager. Grant and the team. Aunt Fay. Saffron. Taffy. Kendall. And even himself.

Though he wasn't entirely sure whether he was pushing or tugging.

He joined Kendall in the sitting room, clueless as to what he might say when he got there.

She was sitting in her usual spot, her hair now pulled back into a high ponytail, her lovely face in stark relief. She let her fingers rest atop the keyboard and pinned him with a steady blue-grey stare as she said, 'I'm ready for dictation, Mr Bennington.'

Hud felt himself wavering. Half wanting to leap over the desk and pull her into his arms and half wanting to turn back the clock and not have encouraged her in the first place. Pressure, pressure, pressure…

He paced over to the couch and sat gingerly on the edge. Through the gap beneath the desk, he watched as Kendall crossed her right knee over her left, swishing her skirt high enough to give him a view of long pale calf. He sniffed in deep through his nose to negate the instant slide of desire moving unimpeded through his body, making a complete mess of his thoughts.

But he couldn't take his eyes off her. Muscles contracting as she bobbed her leg up and down, calves toned by her daily swims. What a leg. Her good leg. Even in a state of out-and-out, down and dirty flirtation, she was still hiding her scars. And he was doing the same. His internal ones at least.

Maybe that was it. That was the way to show her he wasn't the dashing adventurer she seemed to have him pinned to be. Maybe that was the only way to make a clean break. He'd seen the way she'd blanched at the idea of gunshots. The way she had lost breath at the thought of him being impaled on a rusty fence spike. She'd challenged his ability to share. Had accused him of being choked up. And she was right. If she knew the whole truth, then she'd see how human he was too.

'You ready?' he asked.

'As I'll ever be.'

Hud took a deep breath, stretched his neck, closed his eyes and let himself go deep into the real world he'd spent the past weeks staying as far away from as possible.

'That night,' he said, 'the night of the fiesta, Phil, Grant and Vinnie, my semi-regular crew, stayed on at the pub. We weren't due to head out until two days' time when a truck was picking us up to take us to Bogota. But I wanted to check that the fridge in my hotel room was at the right temperature as it had been on the blink before. And it was storing some film from an old camera I had brought with me.'

Kendall cleared her throat and Hud pulled himself out of the deep memory which had begun to feel so real, so close that his skin felt clammy, his face hot, his clothes heavy and rough against his limbs.

He focused on a tarnished silver teaset on the coffee table in front of him. Civilised. Elegant. Familiar. Now just as much a part of his life story as Mirabella, as the view from a plane seat, as the desk he shared with half a dozen other snappers at Voyager's head office. He planted himself squarely in his solid surrounds. And it helped.

'I remember the smell of live chickens. Garbage. Old beer. Decaying vegetables. Rotting wood. Yet over the top of it all the scent of air ripe with coming rain.'

He was close now. So close he waited for the shut-down to come. The obliteration of memory that had smitten him half a dozen times in London when he'd tried talking to professionals. Colleagues. Friends…

'Coming rain,' Kendall repeated, her voice soft, soothing, encouraging. And even more familiar than all of those other pieces of his life put together. Familiar and a cut above real. *Essential*.

He looked over to her then, locked eyes, drew his strength from her, from her ability to share the worst of herself and shine bright through it all.

She smiled, her eyes creased, and she nodded. *Go on*, she said, but not aloud. *You can do it.*

He not only could. He had to. To move forward one way or the other.

'I smell sweat. Male sweat. As someone is about to pass. But they don't pass. They stick close behind me. I turn. I see the swing of an arm. Feel lightning crack across the back of my skull, more pain as my head hits the ground. I taste blood. Metallic, salty, mixed with mud. And then nothing. Darkness. A black hole.'

'Hud,' Kendall said, her forehead creased, her mouth down-turned. Her care for him glowing from her eyes so brilliantly he could feel it settling over him like a warm blanket.

The tangy taste in his mouth, the ringing in his ears, the thunderous pulsing in the back of his head faded away at the sight of her.

His beautiful distraction.

His anchor.

His reason to get through this.

'I woke. I was being dragged, harsh terrain beneath my feet. Ground so slippery it was like fractured glass covered in oil. Air so thin my head felt like it was floating away from my neck. The sound of gunshots split the silence, echoing. My first thought was of avalanches, before I realised how close the gunfire actually was. Then my thoughts turned to the protection of flesh. My flesh. But it was too late. The feel of gun metal pressed against one's forehead is not altogether forgettable. I had been kidnapped.'

'Did they know who you were?'

'Wearing a Voyager press pass is usually as good as wearing a red cross on your back. But I've since been told around two-thirds of the world's kidnappings occur in Colombia.'

'Who did this to you?'

Hud felt himself shrug. 'Local "protectors" wanting in on the action. Somehow believing our presence, our story would lead to the Salinas family making too much money. You have to remember this is a country that has been in the grip of guerrilla warfare since the nineteen-sixties over cocaine. They knew how to do this stuff already. Shifting the target to coffee wasn't all that big a leap.'

'Did they…did they hurt you further?'

'I was in their *care* for eight days. No food. Little water. Hog-tied in a mud hut. Then one day I was found in a Salento alley, unconscious, bleeding from the lip. Let go. Who knows why? I woke in a London hospital with only patches of memory remaining. And that's that.'

It was about then he realised Kendall wasn't typing any more. She was leaning her elbow on the table, her hand over her mouth. Tears pouring down her face.

He stood. Paced away with his back to her. He'd come here purely as a way to do as Voyager had asked while at the same time bending the rules in a way that suited him far better than lying on a shrink's couch four times a week for six weeks.

He'd never expected this. He'd never expected to see what had happened to him through someone else's eyes. Someone who so obviously cared for his well-being. Cared that he came home safe and sound. Cared that he had gravel rash on his ankle. He'd never lived with such intense focused care in his whole life. Had never felt it for another living soul. And suddenly it was all too much.

'Hud, I'm sorry,' she said, sniffing deep and clacking madly on the keyboard. 'Keep going.'

'What's the point?' he shot back, his torment bursting out of him as anger. 'There is no book deal.'

'There's…excuse me?'

'There have been offers, but there is no contract. The very thought of people out there reading about me being dragged through mud by men half my size while I loll helpless as a rag doll doesn't appeal all that much. The idea of you picturing me that way is bad enough.' He ran a rough hand over his eyes. 'I'm not who you think I am, Kendall.'

She ran two brisk fingers beneath her eyes and leant back in the chair and crossed her arms over her chest. 'And just who do you think that is?'

'The guy. The one to take you away from yourself. To ease your conscience. To make you forget about George.'

'What makes you think I want to forget about George? I loved him. He was my best friend. My family. I'll never forget him.'

'So what can you possibly see in me? If you were after a roll in the hay, I've been up for it since day one. And if you're after a boyfriend, then I'm not that guy either. I've been alone my whole life and that's all I know. I've travelled for fifteen-odd years and can't imagine living in one place for more than three months. Someone asked me to once. A woman. One hell of a woman. And I couldn't do it.'

She sniffed again, though by now her cheeks had turned beetroot-red. 'So you've been here marking time. I get it. You're itching to get going and leave this dump. They want you back. So why not just leave now? Better yet, why even come back here in the first place?'

He took a few deep breaths and collected himself before he said anything else he'd regret. Even though he wasn't all that sure he hadn't riled Kendall past the point of doing the same. 'I came back here for some down time, Kendall. And I don't regret a second of it. For then I wouldn't have met you.'

She threw her hands in the air and pushed back her chair with a loud scrape. 'And how different your life would be then! No different, Hud. You'll leave anyway and I'll stay here, with my secure job and my quiet routine, where the brightest part of my day has been a secret swim. And I know there's no book, Hud. You've had no more interest in writing this thing than you have in learning underwater basket-weaving.'

He gawped. He felt it in his cheeks—a full-on, open-mouthed gawp.

She stood and paced behind the desk. 'All I ever wanted was for you to be honest with me. But I'm not altogether sure you have the ability to even be honest with yourself. You go on about your fly-by-night life, no connections, living life from behind your camera lens, but then you talk of Fay and your parents and even big Grant with such tenderness I just know that they all mean far more to you than you even realise.'

'Right. Like you've been so honest with me from day one?'

'Far more readily and easily than you have been with me. Which only proves me the bigger fool. So what am I, Hud? A charity case? Some poor little local to toy with until your down time ran out?'

'Kendall, don't you even think about trying that with me.'

'Or what?' Her cheeks were so pink she looked as if she'd been lying in the sun for a day. And standing there, glaring at him, she infused him with such energy he wasn't sure how to control it.

'Or I'll kiss you again,' he said. 'Or worse. I'll take you in my arms and throw you to that couch and do to you exactly what those big expressive eyes of yours have been telling me you've wanted me to do to you for days.'

'Ha!' she said. 'Don't you think by now I've figured out you're all talk?'

Her eyes blazed, her chest rose and fell with such pace it made him feel breathless himself. Was she pushing him to…?

'All talk and emotionally stunted,' she threw at him so fast he rocked back on his feet. 'I knew it. From the first moment I looked into those great sad hazel eyes of yours I knew it. And it drew me in. Like a fish on a hook. Stupid. Stupid Kendall. I deserved it. All of it. A lesson. That's what you've been to me. A great big important lesson.'

Hud clenched his hands at his sides, stunned to find that he still wanted nothing more than to kiss her senseless. 'Emotionally stunted, am I? I'm not sure that you are ready to hear all that much about the depth of my true emotions right now, Kendall.'

'Try me.'

He'd never wanted to kiss a woman so much in

his life. To strip her down and make love to her until she sobbed his name. Had never felt so much as though if he didn't he might never be able to breathe properly again.

She raised an eyebrow at him as if to say, *Go on, then*. Well, she'd asked for it.

He strolled closer, the deliberate pace belying the frantic beat of his heart, the skipping and tripping nature of his thoughts, the rocketing momentum of his desires. And he said, 'What if I told you that, right now, my emotions have very little to do with some faraway, long ago, short-lived awful experience that far more people are interested in my reliving than I'll ever be, and have far more to do with you.'

She blinked up at him for several moments before poking herself in the chest and seeming genuinely shocked when she said, 'I'd put my fingers in my ears and say la-la-la really loudly until the voices in my head stopped trying to convince me of the same thing. Because I'm over it.'

Hud had had enough. He reached out, took her by the upper arms and pulled her to him. Her skin felt so soft beneath his palms. Her hair smelt of fresh air and the rest of her smelt of pine needles and something wholly her. Something sweet and dark all at once.

She wobbled on her toes and looked up into his

eyes, her own beautiful blue-grey eyes lighting up with dawning recognition. And pure unbridled attraction. And something far deeper, far more hazardous, and far more seductive.

Victory.

CHAPTER TWELVE

HUD's eyes were dark. So dark against the perfect whites. His pupils so large that if Kendall hadn't known their exact colour as well as he knew hers, then she would have guessed they were black.

So beautiful. All she could think were the words so *beautiful*.

He groaned as he held her tight and rained kisses over her neck. 'I crave you, Kendall. Since the second I first saw you I've wanted this. You drive me wild.'

Wild? He thought he wasn't the man she thought he was. Well, that one word showed her how far she was from the woman he thought she was. Maybe at one time, as a young girl trying to get some flicker of recognition from her father, she'd been a tearaway, but that wasn't really her, any more than being a super-controlled whole-some good girl was really her either. The real her lay somewhere in the middle.

'Hud,' she said, disentangling herself from him and pressing her fists against his chest. 'Hud, wait.'

He pulled away, breathing hard and deep through his nose. His eyes were gleaming. His lips moist. And the whole of him just too beautiful for words. Too beautiful for her. Too shiny, too beautiful and, yes, too wild.

He reached out to cup her face and she flinched. Her eyes fluttered and her jaw clenched.

His hand dropped. 'What's wrong?'

Where could she even begin?

She began by sitting on the couch, as her knees were shaking. She rested her hands on her lap and looked down at the beautiful coffee table, knowing she wasn't even wild enough to put her feet upon it.

'I put pen caps back on after use,' she said. 'I look three times when I cross the road. I squeeze my toothpaste from the bottom up so as to get the most out of every tube. If you think I'm wild then I'm not who you think I am either.'

The cushioned seat sank to her left as Hud sat beside her. 'I'm not so different from you, Kendall.'

'Please,' she scoffed. 'You live your life on the edge. You're completely different from me.'

'I don't run into burning buildings. I would never stand in the line of fire to get the perfect shot. I am very protective of my body. I don't want it to be hurt any more than you do. I wear flak jackets when I need to, which has been perhaps eight times in my whole career. In the past year, apart from Colombia, I have photographed villagers in Utah, wildlife of the Zambezi, the insides of fertility specialists' rooms in London, and other such lacking-in-danger places.'

'But Colombia—'

'Was an anomaly.'

'So you are going back.' It wasn't a question.

'I…haven't yet made up my mind. But, even if I did, I wouldn't be able to just walk away from here.' His voice cracked just a little when he added, 'Kendall, I don't want to lose you.' He reached up and rested his palm along her cheek. It felt so warm and so right, she could have purred. 'If we can go one day without going for each other's jugulars, that is.'

'I quite like that part of it, actually,' she admitted. 'Everybody else in my life is so nice.'

'And you're not nice?' he asked, his fingers moving around to the back of her neck, creating tingles down her spine.

'Not altogether,' she admitted.

'You really are the temptress of your lifetime, Ms York.'

'You have no idea how much I love you telling me that, Mr Bennington.'

'Well, then, how about this? What would you think about me basing myself here, at Claudel, rather than my London apartment?'

All jokes and flirtation aside, Kendall's focus shifted and honed in on Hud's mouth. Had he really just suggested…? 'You'd actually move here? Live here? Like on a permanent basis?'

'I could.'

'Meaning you'd be here how often?'

His neck actually turned pink as he said, 'Eight, nine weeks a year.'

Eight or nine weeks? The glorious flush that had brightened Kendall's world for all of fifteen seconds was snuffed out in a tenth of that time.

Eight or nine weeks wasn't nothing. Not when compared with what she had now, and what she would have if she rejected his offer. And it was a sweet offer, really. Coming back here to small town pace, to lazy days and even lazier nights, to a post office where the postmistress knew your business before you did, instead of the cosmopolitan London he was used to.

He must have felt her hesitation, her fading, as he added, 'And perhaps you could meet me over there for some of that time as well. I could show you my London between short gigs. And from there anywhere in Europe is at the end of a ridiculously short plane trip too.'

It was awfully sweet. Awfully tempting. And awfully unfair. For, no matter what platitudes he gave, what quotes he quoted at her, he was wild and beautiful and free and she was trapped inside a body that would never be whole, that would never be able to keep up.

'You have no idea how much I appreciate your offer, Hud. Truly. But it would never work,' she said, kicking herself the moment the words came out of her mouth.

Hud's face closed down. Went from excited to disappointed in a heartbeat. 'Never is a very final kind of word.'

'It is,' she admitted, looking up into his face, taking note of every angle and shadow and flaw to give herself something to hold on to when he left and she never saw him again.

'I can't accept that. When I'm with you, Kendall, everything else just melts away. And I'm sure you feel the same way.'

'Hud, I—'

He held up a hand. 'I…I know I've tried to brush this off several times, but since the incident in Colombia, I have been less than myself. Less able to sleep through the night when I can usually sleep through a hailstorm. Less able to concentrate for long periods. More protective of myself and my space.'

He stopped, swallowed and looked down into her eyes with such fierce need that Kendall could scarcely think what he might be about to say.

'What I'm trying to tell you is; while I was busy protecting my front door you came right in through the back and made yourself at home. I've become accustomed to having you there, nearby, within reach, at my back, and I don't want to lose you.'

And I don't want to lose you, she thought, but she couldn't say the words. They would only put added pressure on the guy, who was being far nicer than she could ever be. He was offering an affair, something far grander than she'd ever pictured she'd find in sleepy Saffron. But now that she'd tasted more, now she knew how deeply her love for him went, it simply wasn't enough.

'Hud,' she said, choosing the least complicated of the million reasons why she had to tell him no, 'eight or nine weeks with a trip to Paris thrown in once a year might have been the answer to all my dreams if I was another kind of girl, but one day they will send you to Colombia, or somewhere like it again… I don't know that I can be with a man and not be sure he'll come home from work each day. I already lost a man I loved and I don't know that I can go through that again.'

'Are you saying you love me, Kendall?'

The guy was far too smart for his own good.

And she was obviously far too rattled to have let that slip. She did love him. She knew she did, and had for days. How could she not? He was everything fabulous and wonderful and rich and exotic and vital.

She took more care with her next words. 'I'm saying that you heading overseas into danger would break me into pieces and I don't want to go through the process of putting them together again. *Again.* Not when I know what that takes.'

'And that's it?' he asked, his voice hard, broken. 'That's your final answer. No persuading?'

'That's the only answer I have. I'm sorry.'

She stood, her knees even wobblier than when she'd sat. She moved over to what had become her desk and closed her laptop and put her things in her bag.

The silence from his corner was deafening.

She turned to find him standing, watching her through hooded eyes. He came to her slowly—achingly slowly. She drew in a deep breath and held it, waiting, hoping he might go down on his knees and beg. That he might find brilliant responses to everything she'd said. Tell her he loved her desperately. To make her believe she could be wild. And free. And beautiful. And strong enough to let him be who he needed to be.

But he simply leaned in and kissed her on the

cheek. Stubble rasping. Bathing her in the scent of sandalwood, which would forever remind her of him. Then he stood his ground, his hands buried deep in his jeans pockets, his mouth a thin horizontal line as he watched her walk away.

Emotionally stunted. Leaving town. Dangerous to her equilibrium and to himself. Everything she'd told herself in the beginning had been wrong with him.

And she'd never been so unhappy with herself for getting the facts so right.

Hud spent the next two days doing what he ought to have done in the first place. Working harder than he had his whole life, until he was dripping with sweat. Cleaning and cataloguing. Pulling off drop cloths and sweeping up dust, and opening creaky windows and letting fresh air and sunshine flood into the house.

The winds of change brought with them the scents of summer. Honeysuckle. Roses. And pine. A scent that would for evermore remind him of a stubborn redhead who had burst through his life like a shooting star. Shining bright. Leaving a lasting impact, but burning out before he really had the chance to know her.

He wondered where she was right now. Sitting at her Formica desk working. Having coffee with

Taffy in town. Swimming in his pool house. He wondered if she would ever go there again. He hoped so. Because he was crazy about her. He'd told her as much, and had been truly shocked that she didn't feel the same way. She didn't love him enough to at least try to see if what they had was worth taking further.

Yet the thought of not seeing her again just made no sense. He wasn't feeling angry, or disillusioned, or any of the things he ought to have been feeling, because he simply didn't quite believe it. He and his mermaid couldn't possibly be through with one another. They'd barely begun.

In the continuation of his mad cleaning jag—which he was smart enough to know was simply a displaced dispersal of tightly coiled emotional energy—in the drawers of Fay's office desk he found treasures he never would have found if he hadn't been working around the clock like a mad man to get this place ready to…leave for another decade? Sell? Move in anyway? Who knew?

Postcards from his parents. As soon as he saw them, wrapped in a red ribbon in a small brown wooden box, he remembered them with as much clarity as if they'd just arrived at the Saffron post office.

He sat and read them. In order. There was at least one a week for every summer he'd spent at

Claudel. Tales of adventure and of discovery, but mostly questions—about him, what he was up to, how much they missed him and hoped they could come home sooner than expected.

One had even come attached to his first ever camera. A gift from his father. With the proviso that he take photos of himself and his own adventures at Fay's. For them.

'Well, I'll be damned,' he said to the walls. For he'd forgotten that entirely. And there was nobody else to tell. Nobody else who would understand their significance. Or the immense weight that had lifted off his shoulders in remembering the important moments that had shaped his life.

Kendall was right. Memory was fickle. Knowing things wasn't anywhere near as powerful as recording them. Books, poetry, plays from hundreds of years ago, love letters, marriage certificates, news articles, diaries, postcards, photographs…

That was the only way memories could truly last past a moment in time. The way meaning could be preserved longer than the time it took for another person to twist it and colour it and flavour it wrong inside their own mind.

He pictured a future in which his likeness became such an image to Kendall. When her memories became a warped version of the time they'd truly had together. Even now, forty-eight hours later, she'd be remembering him wrong.

Kendall *was* right. But not about everything. In that moment Hud's energy found a whole new focus.

'Mail for you!' Taffy called out.

'Bring it here,' Kendall begged from her place on the couch on which she'd practically lived for the past three days.

'Not gonna happen. The letter is addressed to Kendall York, not Ms Sooky Sorry For Herself Couch Potato.'

Kendall picked Orlando up from his place on her belly and put him on the floor before dragging herself off the couch and into the front entrance, where an unstamped envelope bearing her name lay atop a pile of bills Taffy hadn't bothered to mention.

She picked it up, turned it over. No return address. Her father never put the return address on his cards but from him it would have had a stamp.

'Did you pick this up from the post office?' she called out.

'Nope,' Taffy called from the direction of the kitchen. 'I found it slid under the front door.'

Kendall's hand began to shake as she tore open the back of the envelope and shook the contents free. She had no doubt who it was from. If it was a goodbye note…

She slid the contents into her hand. They were photographs. Of her.

She leant her backside against the hall table which rocked hard against the wall but held her suddenly dead weight.

She sifted through the photos of her sitting on the edge of the pool, legs dangling into the water. A soft restful smile on her face, the skirt of her dark green dress scrunched up around her thighs as if she had not a care in the world.

Photos of her eyes. Her feet. Her hands. Her legs looking like a mermaid tail beneath the water. But mostly of her face. Looking down, eyelashes sending shadows over full cheeks. Looking out, the colour of her eyes vibrant from the reflected light from the pool. Looking almost beautiful.

'Jeepers,' Taffy whispered from beside her. Kendall looked up; she hadn't even heard her friend come back.

'When did you get these done?'

Kendall shook her head. 'I didn't. I… Hud. He must have taken them without my knowing.'

'Jeepers,' Taffy said again, this time with reverence.

Kendall ran her finger gently over one picture of her face, the focus on her smile, the rest of her a slight blur. She'd been smiling that day because she'd been thinking of him. Daydreaming. Allowing herself to revel in the possibility of him. It had been a few brief shining moments of bliss. And he'd been there. He'd seen it. And captured it for ever on film.

He'd documented the moment so that she would now never be able to forget it. She swallowed down a lump in her throat.

A slightly raised bump in that one image made her turn the picture. It had been dated and initialled and a note in Hud's long looping hand read:

The most beautiful woman I've ever known.

Kendall felt her eyes fill with tears, just before they completely blurred her vision. She let the hand holding the photo drop, her energy to keep herself held together finally expended.

'Kendall,' Taffy said softly, 'sweetie, are you okay? Is there anything I can—'

'No!' Kendall said so loudly Taffy jumped. 'Sorry. But it's not up to you to do anything. I'm the one who screwed this up. I'm the one who pushed him away. Right at the moment he really needed me. More than any of the other victims I have clung to over the years, trying to absolve myself of what happened to George.'

Orlando whimpered from his spot on the rug in the lounge room as though he'd heard her.

'Sweetie,' Taffy said, 'you know that wasn't your fault—'

'I know!' Kendall closed her eyes, sniffed back her tears and lowered her voice before saying again, 'I know. I do. But it still hurts to know how many people were hurt when he died.'

'There are those of us who hurt when you hurt too, sweetie. All any of us can ask is to be happy. And this last week I have seen you happier than I have in years. Now, don't vomit when I say this, but you've blossomed before my very eyes. You are rosy and smiley when you think nobody's looking, and far easier to push around, which has been a delight for me.'

Kendall smiled through her tears.

'And that's all Hud, isn't it?' Taffy asked.

Kendall nodded. 'Hud, and the things he's made me realise about life, about me, and about…love.'

'God, now I'm going to cry!' Taffy said, though it was too late to stop her; she grabbed a handful of tissues from the hall table and blew her nose.

Kendall's wet grin turned into a half-hearted laugh. 'Don't make me laugh. This is bad. All bad. This man is…heaven and in a grand effort to protect myself to the nth degree I've been a total chump.'

Taffy began to sob—so hard that Kendall reached out and pulled her into her arms to make her feel better.

'So this is another of those twenty-three-year-old single female things you were talking about. Making the best friend feel better when you're the one who ought to be able to fall apart.'

Taffy nodded against her shoulder. 'Aren't you glad you finally came into the fold?'

'I'll be more glad to get out of it.'

At that Taffy pulled away. And sniffed and looked just how Kendall had felt three minutes earlier. Before a plan had begun to form in the back of her mind.

Hud sat on the third bottom step of a curling wrought iron staircase leading goodness knew where, nose buried within the final pages of *Henry V*, and found himself deep in the middle of the part he would have glossed over as a kid as the icky bit. The heart of the proposal scene.

But now, taking the time to read between the lines, the beauty of the language and the differences between King Henry and his French princess were so marked it did indeed make his now softened heart a tad fluttery.

This place hadn't only made him soft, it had made him a Shakespeare-lover. His crew would laugh themselves silly if they ever found out. Maybe he'd keep that his secret.

There was a knock at the door.

He stilled, looked up from his spot and listened with both ears, hoping it might be…

The knock came again. It was the front door. His shoulders slumped in disappointment.

Dog-earing his place, he left the book on the stairs and went to the front door. It took a moment to figure out how to unlock it from the inside as he hadn't used it once since first walking through the double doors a week before.

And opened it to find…

'Kendall.'

She stood before him, resplendent in her usual get-up of tank-top and long skirt. Doc Martens covered in dust from the front drive. Her hair was half pulled back, with tendrils tickling the sides of her lovely face, making her look more like a wood nymph than ever.

She slid a hand to her hip and said, 'I got your mail this morning,' in an almost accusatory tone.

He let his brow furrow. 'Mail?'

Her expression faltered for a second before she looked down at her other hand, in which his photographs were clutched. Smudged with fingerprints, as though she had pored over them a hundred times already.

Hope stirred within him. Expectation. Necessity.

She shook her hair off her shoulders and tilted her chin. 'These photos. They're yours, are they not? You've not yet deigned to show me anything you've ever shot, but I just knew. I mean I was sure. And then the message on the back—'

'You are the most beautiful woman I have ever known,' he said, putting her out of her gorgeous misery.

'Oh,' she replied, all challenge fading from her expression like the sun going behind a fluffy white cloud. 'I…I don't know what to say.'

'Don't say anything. Just so long as you know, then I'm a happy man.'

She nodded. And he knew he'd been right. She hadn't really heard him the other day. His words, his declaration had been half-hearted, cryptic, self-preserving to the end, and not nearly enough for her to know how much she meant to him. Well, thanks to his parents' love for him, he'd been given a second chance and this time there was no way he was going to blow it.

'Did you like them?' he asked.

She swallowed. 'They're…beautiful. Truly.'

'It was all the subject matter, I promise.'

'I haven't felt beautiful in a very long time. You have no idea what a gift this was. You are,' she added, her voice shaking.

She then shook her head, moved from one foot to the other and back again, and he remembered her leg. She must have walked here. And was hot. And uncomfortable. And she wouldn't have come unless she had things to say herself. He hoped against rising hope.

'Are you coming in?'

She nodded and did so, glancing up at his face briefly as she slid past him. Her scent, her very presence washed over him in a swell of great expectation.

She remained in the parlour as he pulled the heavy door closed, heels together, photographs still clutched in her hand.

'Hud, I—'

'Kendall, you—'

They spoke at the same time.

'You go first,' she offered.

'I was going to say I would never have taken any photos that day if it wasn't for you. You gave me that gift. You pushed me, inspired me, got me het up and energised and strong enough to move forward in a way I hadn't been able to in months. I thought that day that taking the photos of you had brought me back from wherever it was I had been. But it wasn't the photos. It was you.'

'That's very sweet—'

He cut her off there. 'I'm not sweet, Kendall.

Don't you go thinking that now. The truth is I'm rough and tumble and stubborn and tenacious. Which is why watching you leave me the other day just wasn't something I could take lying down. And I still won't.'

'I'm here now aren't I?' she said, her voice soft and husky and sexy as hell.

'You are. Which makes me the luckiest bastard on earth. The terms I offered you the other day were rubbish and you were right to walk away. I'm new at this…love stuff. I fear I panicked and tried my very best to screw it up before anything else could.'

'This love stuff?' Kendall asked, picking up on the one word he knew she would the moment he said it. Well, if there was any moment to throw himself on the mercy of the fates, to offer himself up for self-sacrifice, this was it. And the risk was beyond worth it for the reward on offer.

Her.

'If Colombia was a wake-up call that my life was out of control and not in a good way, coming here was like waking up with the sun pouring through an open window. And that had everything to do with you. From the moment I saw you in the pool house, slicing through the water as if I had stumbled upon my very own mermaid, I was captivated. And since that time, as I've come to know you, your big heart, the way you challenge me at every turn, the way you've opened my mind to a new way of looking at the world, I am still to this day stunned.'

He moved to her then. Taking her hand in his. She tucked the photos into the back of her skirt and lay her other hand over his. It was trembling.

'Kendall, I am willing to do what it takes to have you in my life. Because that's the only life I will choose. I am in love with you.'

She swallowed, tears gathering in her wide open eyes.

'I love photography. I love travel. But I love this place. I love the memories encapsulated here. I don't need to work. But I do need to keep busy. Keep inspired. Keep trying new things. And I can always combine my loves without working for Voyager.'

'You're not going to Africa?'

'Not sure. But I did post my resignation letter to London this morning. I may still go to Africa. But only if you come with me. You haven't taken holidays in three years. That's almost three months' worth of leave.'

'How do you know how much leave I have?'

'Taffy told me.'

'Of course she did.'

'Come with me, Kendall.'

She opened her mouth, her head shaking just

once to the left, ready to say, *I can't,* as if it were a habit. But instead she shut her mouth, licked her lips, looked him in the eye, then said, 'I'd like that.'

Without thinking about it, he reached out and scooped her up into his arms. Twirling her around in the wide open space, his bare feet squeaking on the black and white tiled floor, French windows and arched doorways blurring as he whipped past them.

She laughed so loud he felt it reverberating through his chest until he laughed too. He slowed and let her body slide against his.

When she hit the ground, she kept looking up into his eyes, her expression so fuelled by love he knew his trust in his instincts had been spot on.

'I came here to tell you that I am in love with you, Hud. The past couple of days have been miserable. Just ask Taffy the next time she sees you. I'm sure she'd be happy to oblige on the gory details.'

'I will,' he said, smiling down at her.

'I know it's crazy, but I think I've loved you since the moment I looked into your eyes in the pool house. You're like nobody I've ever known. Yet somehow you're just like me. It's like the moment I first saw you I just had no choice.'

'Are you saying you love me because I remind you of you?'

'Could be,' she said with a cheeky smile. 'Or it

could be your seriously sexy arms. Or those hands of yours that do magical things to my bones when they touch me. Though it could always be your kiss. Are you sure you didn't pick up some magic love potion on your travels?'

'If I did, I can assure you there's plenty more where that came from.'

'Then count me in.'

'In?' he asked, faltering at the last hurdle, somehow amazed that this amazing woman was truly smitten by him. With all his faults and flaws and baggage.

'Your life. If you'll have me. I am completely and utterly yours. I choose you, Hud.'

'Well, that's really terribly fortuitous because I am also yours, and have been for some time. I choose you right on back.'

He dropped his chin, let himself savour her breath on his lips for a few moments before pressing his mouth to hers, reiterating everything he said and felt with his kiss.

'I love you, Kendall,' he said when they finally broke apart.

'I love you too, Hud. But don't think that means I'm ever going to back down if you say something I don't agree with.'

'I'm glad. I quite like that part of our relationship. Everybody else in my life is so nice.'

'And you're not nice?' she asked, trailing her finger down his cheek and into the dip where his T-shirt met his clavicle.

'Not even the tiniest little bit,' he said with a growl in his voice.

'Prove it,' she said, and Hud spent the rest of that day, and the next, and the next doing just that.

EPILOGUE

KENDALL stood atop an old battlement in the mountain top town of San Gimignano in Italy.

Her leg ached like crazy from the slow walk up the long hill. She closed her eyes and took a moment to stretch. To breathe.

Then opened her eyes to find herself looking out over the multicoloured hills of pastoral Tuscany. A vision so poetic she lost her words completely.

She'd filled three whole brand-new red note-books over the past three months travelling through Africa and Europe, taking care to record every wonderful detail about all the beautiful things she had seen, knowing her mind would become so full she would forget ninety-nine per cent of it.

And now that word had come through that Voyager Enterprises wanted to buy a series of coffee table books, her hand-written reminiscences scrawled beneath Hud's photographs, her world finally felt as if it had come full circle.

The click and whirr of a professional camera brought her from her reverie. She turned to find Hud—her Hud—standing five feet away, aiming Mirabella at her.

She held a hand up in front of her face. 'Stop it. You're in Tuscany, Hud. There are a billion more interesting things to photograph than me.'

Through her splayed fingers she saw him drop the camera to chest height so that he could look at her more fully.

'Name one,' he said.

She let her hand fall to her side, wishing she had a camera herself. But not even the most brilliant photographer would be able to capture the light wind mussing his dark hair, the vigour in his dark hazel eyes, the years of wear mapped out on his old khaki cargo jacket, or the latent energy coiled just below his skin, reaching out to her, calling to her, sapping her thoughts far more easily than another stunning view.

She swallowed to wet her dry throat before offering, 'Well, that fabulous old outdoor cinema down there, for one. And all those lemon trees. And…'

His long legs brought him to her side in three strides. She stopped talking and wrapped an arm about his waist as he pulled her tight. Snug. Sliding until their bodies moulded against one another.

'What did I ever do to deserve you?' she asked.

'You loved me.'

'That's it?' she asked, still amazed, even after three months spent travelling the world with him, that this was all real. He was real. That he wanted her, and desired her and loved her right on back.

This man. This strapping, adventurous, worldly, beautiful man of hers.

'That's everything,' he said, leaning down to place a soft kiss on the tip of her nose.

As usual such sweet intimacy wasn't enough. He lowered his head further, placing his lips over hers, branding her and marking his place for later. For another night spent in a strange bed, in a strange town, a million miles from where she'd ever thought she'd end up, but in the same pair of strong arms she knew she'd sleep in for the rest of her life.